One Brain Cell

roadbloc

ISBN: 0957063393
ISBN-13: 978-0957063396

For all the drug dealers out there. Keep it up. No matter
what.

CONTENTS

ACKNOWLEDGMENTS

Thanks to my family because I have to and it's expected of me. Thanks to Joe, Sam, Ryan, Tinny and Chris (The I Shower Naked Club) for being okay with this project. Shout-out to Reece and Kristoff for demanding I somehow shoehorn them into the tale. And finally Rouse, Abbie, Josh and everyone else who proof-read and gave me invaluable feedback. Y'all rock. ☺

DAY 1

The apocalypse. Year after year the human race had obsessed with how it would happen. When, where and how was always on the mind of curious imaginations. Would it be global warming? The sun exploding? Would World War Three mop up the remains of civilisation as we knew it? Perhaps an unstoppable comet from outer space or the vengeful finger of God pointing down death to thy sinners. Would it be a quick and unnoticeable affair or a slow and painful reality check as the human race were dragged to extinction unwillingly, kicking and screaming every step of the way?

Ironically enough, it went the way that was probably the most popular and fantasised throughout history. The zombie apocalypse. And perhaps the most ironic thing of all is despite the flooding of zombie apocalypse theories in the media, the endless supply of movies, books, video games, comics and TV shows; when zombies did begin to infect the world, the human race fell flat on its face. There was no stopping the zombies as they infected their way through the globe. Governments collapsed. Armies were overwhelmed. All survivors were eventually consumed or infected. It was certainly a shameful display.

This particular story begins in God's own county, a small number of miles off the edge of a small town called Morrhead. Morrhead was by no means anything special. No streets were paved with gold. The streets were paved with the butts of cigarettes and litter. In fact, other than the endless rows of council estates and derelict buildings, not much had occurred in Morrhead since the industrial revolution.

Four pairs of glassy eyes stared at the television set as competitive store owners and collectors fought over auctioned storage units. The hazy bubble they were in seemed tranquil as the world began tearing itself apart. Ignorance was bliss. That is, until Robin decided to idly glance out of the window.

"Oh... whoa..." he muttered with mild interest as the people who lived in the house opposite ran out of their home, blood soaked, bitten and in horror, "Summats going down outside..."

The three pairs of remaining eyes were dragged from the focus of the television screen to the front window. The neighbours were not having a good time at all as they attempted to orchestrate their rushed and poorly thought out escape plan. Pale and ravenous hands clawed the desperate family from their Ford Mustang. Gnawing mouths, spitting out vowels of disgust, chewed their way through living flesh as the father figure attempted to start the car.

Too little too late as a horde of ten or so zombies swamped the vehicle, dragging the driver through his window and making mincemeat of the two wailing kids in the back seats. The mother saw her chance. Avoiding a bite from another zombie, she switched to the driver's seat, successfully started the car and accelerated over the horde that were attempting to tip and break into the car. There was a squelch and snap of body parts as she mowed through them, through the fence of the garden opposite, narrowly missing Robin's parked car and then into the

2

house wall. A horn blared out as the car caught alight.

"Hell yeah! Zombie apocalypse!" Jeremy roared enthusiastically, jumping up as a poor screaming woman outside was torn to pieces on the pavement by hungry zombies in a flurry of tearing flesh, black blood and snarling teeth.

"No way!" Dustin exclaimed, standing up to see the carnage occur outside. Somewhere, something exploded with an ear ripping bang.

"Yes way, about time!" Shawn cheered, his eyes finally being torn from the auction to the outdoor events. A skeletal and flaming zombie... or was it a human... screamed down the street.

"Oh ye! What are we gonna do?" Jeremy asked, as Shawn and Robin continued to be lazy, "We should make plans!"

"Not until Storage Wars is finished fam," Shawn replied, his eyes returning to the heated auction on the television set.

"Yo fuck that show," Jeremy snorted, watching the carnage occur outside, "We need to do something or we're gonna get eaten fast!"

"Jeremy's right," Dustin said, his eyes wide with horror as he watched a flaming body writhe itself from the burning combination of car and house, "We need to find somewhere safe and with lots of food..."

Reluctantly, Shawn stood up. Robin continued watching TV as though the zombie apocalypse was a figment of his imagination.

"Ohhh myyyy God.... heeelp mee!" somebody screamed as they were chased down the street by an angry horde.

"What sort of zombies are we dealing with?" Shawn asked, stretching slowly as though he had just woken up.

"Left 4 Dead methinks," Dustin responded.

"They're too fast. It has to be Resident Evil," Robin piped up.

"Oh, I was thinking maybe they're possessed," Shawn debated, still stretching, "You know, like in Doom?"

"Na they're deffo dead. Probably DayZ," Jeremy argued, "We need to find an army barracks of some sort."

"Think realistically bro," Dustin urged, "Right now, what have we got?"

"I think they are Left 4 Dead zombies actually... we better hope we don't run into a tank," Jeremy said half to himself.

"Robin's car," Shawn answered as Robin agreed, his eyes still on the TV.

"Any weapons?" Jeremy asked.

"Golf clubs, snooker cues, BB guns... a few knives..." Shawn listed off the potential weapons they had.

"What about food?" Dustin asked as somebody slammed themselves against the living room window in desperation, making the four of them inside jump. The horde behind the poor soul trapped outside dragged him down to the ground, leaving a long smear of blood trailing down the window. Vein popping screams were heard as he hit the ground and out of sight. Dustin closed the curtains, blocking the carnage from view.

"Fridge full of stuff," Shawn replied.

"Any other peeps?" Jeremy asked.

"Just Jack..."

Jack was Shawn's brother. Having done nothing much with his life beyond compulsory education, he spent his remaining days watching movies on his blu-ray player. Fear built up in the four of them as they left the living room approached the pit that was Jack's bedroom, sounds of Batman punching Gotham criminals coming from within.

"Oh thank fuck he's fine!" Robin said when Jack lazed out upon his bedroom sofa watching his high definition movies on his 90s television came into view.

"Thank fuck? I was hoping he had been bitten!" Shawn complained as Jack grudgingly paused his movie and looked at them with a less than impressed look.

"Wot?" Jack wotted obnoxiously, clearly annoyed at his viewing interruption.

"Zombie apocalypse yo, time to hussle!" Dustin said.

"Wot?"

"You deaf?" Jeremy asked, "Zombies have happened!"

"Whatever..." Jack returned to watching Batman waste criminals, clearly not believing their story.

"Oi! Wasteman! You coming or what?" Shawn asked sharply to his brother.

"Do you mind? I'm trying to watch this!" Jack looked pissed off at the continued interrupting of his movie.

"Fine!" Shawn left the room, followed by the rest. Out in the hallway, they could see several zombie bodies clawing at the door. Time was running out.

"Right, me and Dustin will sort out food," Jeremy instructed as the four of them instinctively entered the back room, away from the front door, "You two find any weapons we could use."

"Then what?" Robin asked.

"Then you drive us out of here," Shawn replied, pulling Robin over to a box of junk to search as Dustin and Jeremy burst into the kitchen.

"Where to?" Robin asked to deaf ears as Dustin opened his bag and let Jeremy slide all of the canned food from Shawn's cupboards in. From the front door they could hear the smashing of glass. Time was running out even faster than they'd anticipated and the knives Shawn had in his kitchen would have been lucky to lightly bruise somebody.

Dustin quickly helped Jeremy empty the contents of Shawn's fridge into another bag before the pair of them hurried back into the back room. Robin was still searching boxes and had put two BB guns, a cricket bat, two pool cues and a large golden Buddha ornament upon the table. Shawn was in the hallway retrieving his golf clubs. He returned with only two of them as the sound of more glass shattering and wood splintering came from behind him.

"Is this it?" asked Jeremy as the four of them looked upon their dismal choice of weapons.

"I guess we're all fighting over the cricket bat then," said Dustin.

"Fight all you want, I'm just taking it," replied Shawn, picking it up.

Before Dustin could react, Jeremy and Robin had swiped a pool cue and a golf club each.

"Aw, fuck, seriously guys?" Dustin moaned as he viewed the remaining weapons. Two BB guns that were most likely useless against zombies and a fat golden Buddha. There was only one choice. Or maybe two.

Hearing the sound of the front door buckling inwards, Dustin grabbed the Buddha and a BB gun. Slipping his rucksack of food on his back, he nodded towards the back door at the end of the kitchen. It was time to get out.

Once they were all inside the kitchen, Shawn locked the kitchen door to buy them a few more seconds. Riddled with nerves, they stared door as though mentally daring each other to be the one to open it first.

"Bloody frosted glass," Dustin snarled, "We can't see if the damn garden is safe!"

"Fuck it," Jeremy grabbed the large nail that was acting as a replacement door handle and swung the door open. Sunlight poured into their eyes, blinding the four of them for a horrible moment. The split second of vulnerability gave way to relief as their eyes adjusted to the light and they found the garden as overgrown and empty as usual. Behind them they could just hear the front door finally giving way and the sound of zombies tumbling into the hallway.

"What about Jack?" Robin asked as Jeremy peered round the house to check if the way to Robin's car was clear.

"What about him?" Shawn replied. It seemed Shawn didn't like his slob of a brother much.

"Coast is clear... ish," said Jeremy.

"Ish?" asked Dustin as the sound of dead fists banging against the kitchen door startled him. The four of them jumped out of the house and closed the door.

"About three walkers left, I think most of them were caught up in that car crash and the rest are probably behind us watching Storage Wars."

"Don't call them walkers, that's unoriginal," Dustin replied.

"Then what should we call them?" asked Robin as they all peeked round the corner of the house to see the said 'three walkers' themselves.

"Zombies."

"Yeah, because that's so original too," Shawn rolled his eyes.

"Left 4 Dead AI?"

"The way is clear... now!" Jeremy cut the debate short and ushered them out. Gripping their rudimentary weapons with hot and sticky hands, the four of them slipped round the side of Shawn's house and sprinted across the blood-soaked and wreckage ridden road towards Robin's black Fiat. Shawn batted away a limping and armless lumbering zombie as Dustin almost tripped over the remains of somebody on the road. They felt a moment of relief when they reached the car unscathed.

"Phew!" breathed Jeremy. Dustin glanced at Shawn's house. The front door was down and unaware zombies were still pouring into it.

"Fuck." It was Robin. He was staring at the front of his car. It turned out, the neighbors Mustang on its final voyage had inadvertently caused a large amount of house debris to crash down upon the engine. Below the crumpled mess that had once possibly been a bonnet, a sticky pool of oil had collected. The car was not drivable.

"Fuck," Shawn repeated Robin's words, wiping blood off his bat as the reality of their situation hit home. The armless zombie was staggering towards them for another attempt at eating them and its hungry moans was attracting the attention of other and more agile eyes. Their plan was failing already.

"Fuck," Dustin repeated Shawn's words.

"Oh shit, what now?" Jeremy asked.

"Oh man, I'm going to have to get this to the garage somehow-"

"Fuck the garage Robin!" Dustin snapped, "It's the zombie apocalypse, we need to live."

"We need to move out of here fast," said Jeremy as he rammed his golf club into the chest of the armless zombie. It toppled over and writhed uselessly on the floor, decorating the tarmac with more red. A few of the zombies that had entered Shawn's house were now quickly approaching.

"Coniston?" Dustin suggested, "We can see Morrhead center from there and hopefully it'll be quiet."

They all silently acknowledged that Coniston was the best place to go. It wasn't far from their current location, but annoyingly uphill all the way. However, going uphill was better than being eaten, so they all sprinted off up the road. The crossroads ahead of them was quite busy. Cars were pushing through in all directions as the people of Morrhead scurried about in panic like worker ants on fire. Limbs and mechanical wreckages were strewn everywhere. As they all approached the road, Dustin uselessly firing BB pellets a zombie that was chasing them from behind, a burning truck deliberately crashed straight into Dave's corner shop. The drivers leaped out and straight into the shop to loot, both wearing balaclavas and waving makeshift wooden weapons. Unfortunately for them, their plan had attracted the attention of a screaming zombie horde. The four of them heard the sounds of fear and pain from the shop as they ran across the road.

The lone zombie that was chasing them had caught up to Dustin and was attempting to take a chunk from him. Without even thinking, Dustin grabbed the heavy

Buddha from his jacket pocket and lashed out hard, clunking the zombie right upon his or her temple. The soft flesh and bone dented inwards and the zombie collapsed to the ground just in time to be run over by a speeding car. Feeling the weight of all the canned food he was carrying on his back, Dustin pushed on, catching up.

After about five minutes of uphill running beyond the busy crossroads, they found themselves running through the children's park and observing the zombie children make mincemeat of the non-zombie children as they ran. One of the children ran up towards them, but Shawn kicked them away, unsure if that particular child was a flesh eating zombie or a terrified child expecting help off some young adults.

Coniston was a large recreational patch of grass perched on top of a hill that overlooked the center of Morrhead, opposite Fortress Mound. It also had a graffiti covered metal bench. Someone had scribbled the word 'Pesk' all over it. Finally, there was a pile of discarded plastic bottles that acted as nature's rubbish bin. The four of them flopped on the bench upon arrival, gasping for breath. Neither of them had run with such haste before. Fortunately, Coniston appeared devoid of any un-dead life forms.

Unfortunately, Morrhead center was quite the opposite. They all stared in slight horror as they saw the sun lightly bask the carnage below them. The Crystalgate shopping center was ablaze, the orange flames licking the blue sky as black smoke billowed upwards as the fire engine attempting to control the flames also caught fire. The ring road was filled with wrecked cars and corpses, some walking about aimlessly and others reduced to nothing but a bloody smear in the tarmac. An upturned ambulance was still wailing to itself in the center of a nasty pileup. The train station looked like something out of a war zone, immobile headless bodies scattered all about St. George's square as though some sort of execution had taken place.

"Shit... it's Black Friday all over again," said Jeremy, his eyes wide as he slumped on the bench.

"We'll have to call this Zed Wednesday or something," muttered Shawn.

"Last spliff anyone?" Dustin asked, pulling out the apparent last spliff. It was slightly flattened thanks to the unloading of canned foods into his bag.

"Save it bro," advised Jeremy, "We need to focus or we'll end up bitten. We all need to decide, right now, where we're going to go."

There was a pause as they each racked their brains as to where they could go.

"KFC?" suggested Robin.

"No, we need somewhere safer than KFC."

"Middle of the moors somewhere?" Shawn asked.

"Too remote," said Dustin, "We need somewhere safe and out of the way, but also close enough to civilization so we actually have some places with food nearby."

"Shame there are no military bases nearby," Jeremy sighed as the carnage below them all continued.

"Even if there was we probably wouldn't be allowed in still," Shawn pointed out.

"Got it! Carpathian Mills!" Dustin grinned like a madman.

The rest thought about Dustin's suggestion for a moment. The Carpathian Mills were in Sinthwaite. Once old and derelict, the place had since been renovated into a spa and apartments. It would be easily defendable and a convenient short walk away from the village center and the remains of civilization. The only problem was, Sinthwaite was over six miles away.

"How do we get there? Canal footpath?" asked Jeremy.

"That's farce," moaned Shawn at the thought of traveling by foot some more.

"Yeah," agreed Robin, still gasping for breath.

"Canal footpath makes sense, it's the quickest and most direct route."

"And we can shove any zombies into the canal easy," said Jeremy.

"Wait, we're not doing this are we?" Shawn continued to moan.

They did do it. In a fashion. After another few minutes of discussion, the four of them found themselves sprinting through the carnage of Morrhead center towards the canal. All they had to do was cut through the Crystalgate shopping center, and then they'd be relatively safe. Or so they thought.

The grey and dark brown hues Morrhead were being gradually replaced with red. Rivers of blood trickled down the streets and into drains. Luckily for the group, most of the zombies were preoccupied with chasing or eating somebody else, enabling them to approach the burning shopping center unmolested. Outside the Crystalgate shopping center, they all took a cautious breath.

"This is it..." said Dustin as the screams of burning and bitten bodies drifted out from within.

"Think Left 4 Dead. Never stop moving," Jeremy advised.

Neither Shawn nor Robin looked very happy.

"Better hope there are no special infected," Shawn grumbled as Robin patted out a falling ember that threatened to burn his hoodie.

"Let's do this!" Jeremy pulled the back entrance to the shopping center open and the four of them climbed in.

They plunged into smoky corridor after smoky corridor, not once stopping as they coughed and spluttered along. A mindlessly flailing zombie exiting a small office, was dealt with a swift golf club and cricket bat combo to the head. Dustin felt somewhat lost without a real weapon and he hoped that carrying a Buddha would at least get him extra Zen.

Two breathless flights of stairs and a few more stumbling dead bodies later and they had reached the shopping part of the building. It was in an unbelievable state as an almighty fire in the center of the centre licked at an already collapsing roof. Then, just as they had gathered their bearings and were about to cross the shopping center to the main entrance, the collapsing roof finally gave. A nasty sound of screeching metal accompanied by the roof collapsing inwards, crushing all; dead or alive in the center of the mall with large panes of glass roof, huge metal girders and plaster. Dustin could have sworn he caught a glimpse of somebody's head being taken clean off by a falling sheet of glass.

The alarm stopped, leaving a deathly silence as the last few stones toppled upon the mountain of collapsed building before them. A cloud of plaster dust gently brushed by them as they inspected their blocked exit and failed plan with dismay. Shawn swore.

"What now then lads?" Robin asked, inspecting the damage done. The Crystalgate shopping center was going to need some serious renovating. The main exit and vast majority of shops were now crushed under six foot of rubble. Another five steps and they would have been easily crushed by it.

Dustin glanced around. Their choices were slim. The way they had entered was now blocked with many walking dead people, all in search for fresh blood. Beyond that they had the choice of attempting the climb the rubble to the broken ceiling, a small museum that nobody ever entered and a Pear Store which was usually packed full of fruit eating computer lovers.

"We should climb to the roof," said Jeremy with certainty. The certainty left his voice when zombies began aimlessly wandering down from the roof and over the rubble towards them. They were trapped.

"Goddammit, how did they even get up there?" Dustin despaired, "Where now?"

"Pear Store?" Robin suggested, "I could check out the new dPhone 6X-"

"I doubt there is an app that actually helps us kill zombies dude," criticized Shawn, "The museum will hopefully have some decent weapons."

The museum it was. Despite having lived in Morrhead for their entire lives, not one of them had ever entered the museum. Until now. They had no idea what sort of museum it was.

One of the more noticeable things was how small the museum was. The history of Morrhead wasn't the most extensive or exciting. The four of them crept quietly past a display about burning witches that looked like it had been made by the local primary school, while hoping to not attract the attention of the growing numbers of zombies from the destroyed mall center.

"Pills here!" Jeremy jokingly called as he kicked an empty pill bottle across the floor. It rattled along the floor surface louder than expected.

"Nice one!" Dustin hissed sarcastically as the zombies outside began poking their derpy faces in with curiosity.

Shawn swore once again, this time under his breath as the curious zombies began to follow them in slowly.

Their tour of the museum was almost already complete. Stood in-between a suit of armor and sword trapped in a glass cage and one of the most pathetic gift shops in existence, the four of them instinctively ducked down behind a display about the demolition of old mills to avoid being spotted by entering zombies.

To their dismay, instead of wandering around the museum in the correct direction, the five or so zombies that had entered had decided to spread out in all directions. The small circular tour of Morrhead's short and stale history was now surrounded by approaching dead people.

"Goddammit!" Dustin cursed, putting a sweaty forehead into equally sweaty hands. They were trapped.

Without even thinking or even warning anybody, Jeremy smashed the glass cabinet, sending shards of glass shattering loudly upon the floor. Now with the zombies' full attention and the gap between living and dead tissue closing, Jeremy jumped behind the suit.

"Yo, what'ya doing?" Shawn asked casually, his voice not really reflecting the desperation of their situation.

"The only thing we can do," replied Jeremy, climbing into the suit of amour with difficulty as the distance between them and certain living death closed to under a meter, "You guys might want to get behind me."

They obeyed as Jeremy fought himself into the metal suit of armor. Inside, he found the suit to be horribly claustrophobic and stiff. He creaked about on the spot for a moment, like the poor un-oiled tin-man.

"Jeremy, if you're going to do something, do it now!" Dustin instructed as they all backed away from the oncoming horde, their minds pleading for an escape route.

Grabbing the long sword with both hands, Jeremy swung the lethal blade through the air clumsily, almost decapitating Robin.

"Shit man," Jeremy panted, "All this metal is heavier than it looks! And I can't see shit in this thing! I can't breathe!"

The zombies had now reached them. Shawn and Robin began defending themselves with the golf club and cricket bat. Dustin quickly packed the BB Gun into his bag, grabbed one of the snooker cues Jeremy had dropped and helped attempt to fight back the horde.

"Here we go!" yelled Jeremy, having gotten his fight back. The other three stepped back and ducked as he powerfully swung the blade around, slicing through several zombies. Unfortunately this didn't stop them coming.

"Go for the legs!" yelled Dustin at the exact same time Shawn shouted, "Go for the head!"

In confusion, Jeremy swung the sword high and then low, decapitating one zombie and de-legging another, immobilizing both. Conjuring up all the might he could, he continued his rampage upon the oncoming hordes, sending sharp steel, blood and limbs flying in all directions as the rest cowered behind in an attempt to not get bitten.

Unfortunately, the amour was stifling. It had taken its toll on Jeremy's speed. Within seconds he found himself swamped as over a dozen zombies flung themselves upon him. Almost slipping on broken glass, Dustin leaped up to the display that had once contained the suit of armor to avoid being bitten. Shawn and Robin pushed the zombies away from them and onto the shielded Jeremy. With at least ten pairs of undead hands pushing him about, Jeremy lost his balance and fell to the floor with a metallic crash.

The rest cursed as their only chance of fighting the horde was swamped. However, Jeremy was still on the case. On his back and under many rotting legs, Jeremy grabbed for the sword with desperation as Dustin forced his snooker cue through the eyeball of a zombie. The cue sank right through the zombie's head with an awful squelching sound whilst Jeremy lobbed off the legs of any of the horde, allowing Shawn and Robin to finish them off.

As quick as the fighting had started, it finished. Dustin looked around at the carnage before his eyes. Jeremy was still on the floor in his armor and a pool of blood and body parts. Both Shawn and Robin were covered in blood and also looked utterly horrified at the scene in front of them. Somewhere a zombie limb was attempting to move and was slapping repetitively into the blood. Other than that and the noise of screams and destruction from outside, the interior of Crystalgate was silent.

"Is that all of them?" Robin broke the almost silence.

"Think so," Jeremy grunted from the floor as he slowly fought his way out of the bloody amour.

Once Jeremy had gotten out of the amour, the four of them wandered back out of the dull museum. The entrance of Crystalgate and their way to the canal was still crushed under a pile of rubble that was once the roof.

"Do we have to backtrack and go the long way?" Shawn asked in a grave tone.

"Probably not," Dustin replied, scrutinizing the rubble, "I don't think it should be too hard to climb over this junk."

"Ladies first then," Shawn joked.

Dustin pushed himself up over the rubble and onto the broken roof of the mall. Outside, it was still a beautiful day if you looked beyond the tsunami of violence that was occurring within the center of Morrhead. Squinting in the bright sunlight of the blessed summer day, Dustin could make out that the public library had been raided by the local chav residents who must have mistaken books for some sort of food source. Many copies of Harry Pothead were burning beautifully in the sunlight. Many shops were broken or burning, many dead people were up and walking and many people were on the roofs of buildings waving for help to any supernatural and all-knowing being that could possibly be above. Or helicopters.

"Whoa…" Jeremy breathed, looking breathless as he scrambled to the only patch of stable roof before lending Shawn and Robin a hand up.

"Crystalgate Lane road looks sorta clear," said Robin, pointing it out. He was right. Crystalgate Lane was clear with the exception of a totally demolished house that blocked vehicle access and it lead almost straight to the canal. From then on it would be a walk in the park. Or a walk along the canal at least.

"Sounds like a plan," nodded Shawn, watching a grey Renault Clio race around the Morrhead ring road, squashing bodies before shooting out of sight.

None of them however got the chance to move. Their situation changed dramatically within a split second. Not one of them had noticed the aeroplane in the sky from behind. But they did notice it when it seemingly spontaneously combusted. With a bang, the huge passenger plane roared over them, ablaze and disintegrating, dropping of pieces of flaming shrapnel as it plummeted steadily downwards. Had it swooped over them any closer they'd have been blown off the roof.

With a fierce whining sound the plane nosedived straight into Didl Superstore, engulfing foodstuffs and looters in a huge ball of orange flame and clouds of black smoke. The explosion that occurred on impact shook the ground violently, almost knocking the four of them off their feet as the roof continued its slow collapse.

"Whoa..."

All of the aeroplane commotion had attracted the attention of the zombies. As the four of them stumbled about upon the slowly dissolving roof, they saw an overwhelming number of zombies from all directions sprint towards the burning crater that had once been a supermarket. It was the fastest pilgrimage of dead flesh they had seen as the zombies raced towards the wreckage, their dead lungs screaming every step of the way like the damned choir of Satan himself. It was a horribly chilling sight.

Jeremy was just about to suggest they get clear of the roof before it crumbled when a speeding school bus was caught up in the moving zombie horde. Skidding out of control, the driver attempted to regain control of the bus as he pummeled through zombies. It was in vain. Tyres slick with blood, the bus screeched sideways, colliding with the front of the Crystalgate entrance, giving the roof the last remaining excuse it needed to fully collapse.

"Jump!" yelled Dustin, pointing at the bus roof. They jumped just as the roof left their feet and fell down to the bus roof.

The impact was hard. Dustin had to struggle not to continue sliding off the bus roof. Unfortunately for Robin, there was not enough bus to grip. He slid straight off the bus roof and down to the remains of the street below.

With all the commotion occurring, it too Dustin a few seconds to realize that the irritating noise in his ear was actually the bus horn blaring away. It wouldn't be long until it began attracting the zombies back to their location. It was time to move.

"In here!" called Jeremy, who had accidentally opened a roof entrance into the bus when he grabbed out to stop himself from sliding off. Dustin and Shawn piled in without a word, not even thinking about poor Robin, who had landed awkwardly on the ground.

"Aw fuck! That's horrible!" Shawn turned his nose up at the smell and sight of bus interior.

It was filled with dead bodies of children, no older than ten, in nearly every seat. They were all chained up by their ankles so they couldn't escape. Some of them were moving, although it was clear that they were zombified. Blood was smeared everywhere. The smell of rotting flesh was near putrid. His eyes watering, Dustin gipped, forcing himself not to hurl. He had no idea what had occurred in the bus and didn't want to. It was time to get away from the center of Morrhead.

Robin was tapping at door, glancing behind him nervously at the handful of zombies behind him that were approaching the bus with casual zombie-like interest. Without a word as Jeremy joined them in the bus of death, Dustin ripped the very dead driver's head from the horn, opened the bus doors and dragged him out.

"What you doing?" Robin asked, rubbing his knee as Dustin dropped the driver on the cracked tarmac.

"We're driving out of here, c'mon," Dustin replied, jumping in the driver's seat of the bus and placing the weighty bag on his back upon the lap of a dead ginger kid wearing a Tokémon t-shirt.

"Wait, what happened to taking the canal?" Jeremy asked.

"Yeah, do we really want to stay in this bus?" Shawn added, still looking disgusted at the rows of dead children all chained to their seats.

"You know how to drive this, right?"

"Bus drivers can do it, can't be that hard," spat Dustin dismissively, closing the doors before the zombies could reach them, "Hold on."

He started the bus. It took two attempts before the engine finally stuttered to a start. Crunching gears, Dustin sent the bus speeding backwards into the World of Carbs opposite Crystalgate's entrance. Ignoring the crunch of metal and brickwork and skulls from behind, he accelerated forwards again, pummeling straight into a fresh set of angry zombies that had just sprinted out of the broken entrance of Crystalgate. After a moment of bumpiness and blindness as the bus crushed several dozen reanimated dead bodies, Dustin had the bus spluttering away down the ring road.

"That could have been close," Jeremy breathed, gripping one of seats for balance, an eye of caution upon the immobile child's body slumped there.

"It isn't over yet," said Dustin, attempting to mentally retrieve all of the driving knowledge he had learned pre-zombie apocalypse as he narrowly avoided a pileup of smoldering cars.

"What even happened here?" Robin asked, staring with dismay at the rows of dead children bouncing up and down in their seats.

"Fuck knows," Shawn replied, "Tunes?"

"I ain't got my dPod," Dustin frowned, reaching over to the radio controls, "Hopefully somebody out there will still be playing something decent, I can't be arsed with an emergency broadcast."

"Yehman put Crapital FM on," Jeremy suggested.

"Did you seriously just suggest that?" asked Shawn, pulling a disgusted face at Jeremy.

"I bet you it'll be the only one playing tunes!"

Dustin tuned into Crapital FM. Jeremy was right. It was playing music, although Dustin debated whether it could seriously be called music. The simplistic beats of Jay Jessy and I.Am.Will blasted through the bus speaker system. Robin began singing along.

As he turned onto Scar Lane, Dustin noticed the sun was setting at an alarming rate. The day was nearly over. They weren't even halfway to the Carpathian Mills and they needed to be there ideally before the light fully faded. Other than the occasional independently moving limb, the roads seemed fairly clear.

"Good evening Morrhead and that was Jay Jessy and I.Am.Will featuring German-Shepard with 'Party All Summer.' We'd like to take some time right now welcoming a new demographic to the station tonight, the newly birthed zombie race that will no doubt become the hottest new trend. Trust me on this guys, it's going to be bigger than selfies and twerking. Twatter has already exploded with hashtag-zombie and it doesn't look like it'll be letting up soon."

"Actually fuck this station," Jeremy changed his mind upon hearing the moronic DJ.

Dustin didn't need another excuse to change station. As they bounced along the crumbing tarmac of Scar Lane, he turned the tuning dial to find something better.

"Yo, roads blocked!" Robin pointed out.

Dustin looked up. He was right. There was a wall of cars, chunks of broken building and silhouetted bodies blocking access to the end of Scar Lane. They would have to loop around the Gullum clock tower and rejoin the road at the opposite end of the village. Without even bothering to brake, Dustin took a hard right turn, almost tipping the bus over as it curved the sharp corner at nearly thirty miles per hour. Robin lost his grip and fell to the floor.

"…now on Crapital we want to hear your zombie stories. How has the new era affected you? And if it hasn't affected you, can you imagine what it would be like if it had? Get on Twatter and tell us with hashtag-Crapital. Here is some of the Twats we've had so far. Katie from Southampton thinks it's a 'sorry state of affairs.' Terry from Scunthorpe thinks that 'it isn't.' And Liam from Puddock 'is trapped and surrounded by them, oh my God, help me, help me.'

And we'll be right back to you after this short ad break..."

"Fucksake! Crapital is the only damn station on air!" Dustin cursed, switching on the headlights so he could see the road. The road was flooded with bright white light, making a large zombie standing in the middle of the road visible.

"Fuck!" yelled somebody loudly as Dustin attempted to avoid the zombie. Unfortunately he was going too fast. They crashed straight into the fat zombie; the bus rocking violently as meaty limbs jammed mechanics. The bus span out of control and plummeted straight into the Gullum old folks home.

One crash may have been enough for this unusually tenacious school bus to withstand. But two was too much. As their minds slowly crawled back to reality, the engine combusted and parts of building began to collapse.

Realising the seriousness of their situation, Jeremy forced himself up. Both Shawn and Robin appeared relatively unscathed despite being dazed. Dustin however was still slumped in the driver's seat, moments away from being set ablaze.

Using every bit of momentum he had, Jeremy rushed to the front of the bus and pulled Dustin from the seat.

"On your feet soldier! We, are, leaving!" he yelled, slapping Dustin to bring him back to reality.

"Soz Captain Price," Dustin retorted, grabbing his bag of tinned food and forcing himself to the back of the bus.

Shawn smashed the back window and they all jumped out of the burning bus into fading light of the outdoors. The street lamps were inactive and they were still quite far away from their desired destination. Things were beginning to look bleak.

Jeremy was just about to suggest something when the unthinkable happened.

The Gullum clock tower positioned at the end of the street struck nine o'clock. As if a crashed bus wasn't enough noise to attract the zombies, now the clock tower behind them was chiming loudly.

"Goddammit!"

The howling horde of angry dead bodies screamed towards them from all directions, attracted by the clock tower at the end of the street. The idea of going to the Carpathian Mills was now redundant. There was no way they'd be able to fight this horde and even if they did, venturing the rest of the way on foot wasn't a very appealing idea. It was time to think of a backup plan. And fast.

"Quick into Tommy's!" Jeremy yelled, running down a driveway two houses away.

Dustin's eyes lit up. Tommy's house. Their drug dealer friend from Gullum. He didn't know why he hadn't thought of it himself. It would be a perfect place to crash until the heat died down.

Avoiding rage filled swipes from the first ranks of the horde, Dustin, Shawn and Robin followed Jeremy into Tommy's house. To their surprise, the front door was unlocked. As quietly as they could, the four of them slipped in.

Relative silence followed. Or at least it felt like silence, despite the noise of the clock tower and the zombie horde outside. The polite chimes of bells and the deathly howl of the undead were unsettling. Dropping his Buddha down from his pockets, Dustin reached for the last spliff once again.

DAY 2

Tommy's house was completely abandoned. Their night there was eventless despite the commotion occurring outside. After ensuring Tommy's house was secure, they quietly ate tinned food and then attempted to get some sleep. The reason for Tommy and his family's disappearance was a mystery, other than the obvious zombie apocalypse reasons. But there appeared to be no sign of any struggle, no trace of panic, no effort to even pack some things. The house was deserted, though the back door was open and Tommy and his family had obviously vacated without packing.

Trying to sleep was a waste of effort. The harrowing noises from the undead outside was far from soothing and with the clock tower striking and enraging the zombies every three hours, Dustin, Jeremy and Robin spent most of the night laying awake. Only Shawn somehow managed to drop off, and spent the night irritating everything alive and undead by snoring his tits off. With little desire to sleep and with no electricity, Dustin found the night both creepy and boring. Finally when the clock tower struck six in the morning, he decided it was time to do something constructive. And it wasn't long until everyone, even

Shawn, joined him.

Dustin was cooking breakfast from the remains of their tinned food and the countrywide gas reserves as the rest sat around Tommy's dining table. Despite thinking they took a lot, their supplies were running short already.

"I think we should stay here," said Jeremy as he munched on tinned sausage, "Moving about some more will only get us in more trouble."

"But I thought Carpathian Mills were safe," Robin protested.

"Getting there won't be though," Jeremy pointed out.

"What happens when we run out of food?" Dustin asked, "We have about four meals left here at most. I suppose we could scavenge Gullum, but even then, if we do survive, food will eventually run out. We may have a week here at most."

"Suppose we could deal with that when it happens?" Shawn suggested.

A silence followed Shawn's suggestion. It was a silence of agreement. They were staying. For now at least. The first thing to do was draw up a list of jobs that needed to be done.

Job one was defense. Tommy's house was stripped of most its furniture to be used for re-enforcements. All exterior doors and windows were boarded up the best they could with the resources they had. A hammer and nails would have been a godsend, but unfortunately all they could find was a tube of no-more-nails under the kitchen sink. So after a couple of hours of holding up broken pieces of furniture against windows and doors, the house was finally secure-ish.

Despite the seriousness of their situation, the morning seemed pleasantly warm and mostly quiet. In contrast to the previous night, there were very few zombies on the street and the majority of them stumbled past the house with little interest. Any excuse to have a break was used, and since they hadn't much clue what to do now they had barricaded the house, both Dustin and Shawn declared it time for a cup of tea and a few of Tommy's biscuits whilst running water and gas was still available.

"I'm calling shotgun on Tommy's room," said Dustin out of the blue, kicking off the inevitable bedroom war.

"Fine I'll have his mum's room then," Jeremy immediately securing himself the second double bed.

"You can fuck off if you think I'm going on the sofa," Robin moaned, "You can't call shotgun on bedrooms Dustin-"

"I think you'll find he can," Shawn interrupted, "I'll have the spare room then."

"No you can't-"

"Zombie apocalypse changes everything Robin!" bellowed Jeremy, "Shotgun rules apply to a lot of things now!"

Robin looked less than impressed at the thought of not having a room of his own, "Nah fam, this ain't fair-"

"Tell you what, I'll have the sofa and you can have his mum's room," Jeremy offered, "I don't think I want to be in her bed if she returns."

"Nice one bro."

A moment of silence passed and then Jeremy changed his mind again.

"Actually, no, I want the bed thinking about it."

Dustin finished his brew and stood from the kitchen table.

"Oi, poomplex," Shawn frowned, "Where you off?"

"To make my bed, derkhead," Dustin retorted as he slowly strode upstairs, "I'ma put some traps and defenses in there too just incase."

"Soz-hard wasteman."

"Yo, that's actually a good idea," Jeremy quickly followed suit, grabbing his long-sword on the way. It wasn't long before Shawn had gulped his tea down and decided to work on his room, leaving poor Robin downstairs alone, looking at the sunken sofa that was to be his post-apocalypse bed. It could have been worse.

After the three of them prepared their rooms, the decision was made not to be so harsh on Robin. One of them with a double bed, either Dustin or Jeremy, would have to share with him. The only problem was how to decide who would suffer the awkwardness of sharing a bed.

"Swap rooms with you Shawn," said Jeremy as they stood on the landing figuring out a way to decide.

"Oh so now he wants a single bed he knows there is half a chance he has to share his double," sneered Shawn.

"Don't be farce, yo!"

"Stop changing your mind, yo!"

"How about quartz, parchment, shears?" Dustin joked.

"Wot?"

"Rock, paper, scissors!"

"Best of three though," said Jeremy.

"Nah get it over with, just once," Shawn argued.

"Fine."

So it was decided. Rock, paper, scissors was to deliver the verdict. The pair slammed their fists down in the air three times and picked an option. Dustin was about to pull out two fingers in the shape of scissors as Jeremy revealed his rock shaped fist, when he noticed something above him dangling down from the landing roof. It was a piece of string. Looking up, he noticed a hatch on the ceiling he hadn't noticed previously.

"Ha!" ha'd Jeremy, smashing his rock fist into Dustin's scissor fingers, "I win!"

"Anybody checked up there?" Dustin asked, pointing at the hatch above them.

"Um... nope," said Shawn, staring at it in fascination.

"Yo, Robin!" Jeremy called, "You checked out the attic?"

"Na fam!" Robin's voice floated up from downstairs.

He was still sulking on the sofa.

"Maybe that is where Tommy and his family are hiding," Dustin suggested.

"You'd have thought they'd have heard us by now," Shawn pointed out.

All thoughts of who would be sleeping where and with who were dropped. They had an un-searched room to explore. Once they had coxed Robin back to the group, the hatch was opened, dropping down a set of ladders up to Tommy's attic.

The smell of Tommy's attic was a familiar one. The stench hit them before they had even reached the top of the ladder. And once in the attic, the possibility on their mind was confirmed.

There were about a dozen Marijuana plants, basking beautifully in the morning sunshine that was pouring through the attic window. Complete with a small set of weighing scales, a games console, a pile of video games, a few books and even a camp bed. It was Tommy's little secret hideout that he must have somehow kept secret from the rest of his family.

"Wow, I had no idea he grew his own," said Jeremy, staring at the plants with awe.

"Me neither."

"I always thought that his stuff was unique," commented Shawn, feeling one of the green leaves between his fingers gently as Dustin inspected the pile of video games.

"At least Robin doesn't have to sleep on the sofa or with Dustin anymore," said Jeremy.

"Thank fuck we haven't got any electricity, he only has them crappy football games they re-release every year," Dustin scoffed, flicking though the pile of games and books, "But hey, he has 'The Very Hungry Stoner.' Class book."

"What happens in that one again?" Robin asked.

"The stoner is hungry, so he eats and eats and eats

and eats and eats. And then he wraps himself in a sleeping bag. Then in the morning he's in his suit and ready to go to work. The end."

"Oh yeah."

The discovery of the attic and Tommy's plants was a cause for debate for the four of them. As Dustin used more of their tinned supplies and the food from Tommy's cupboards for lunch, the debate what to do with their lives next was taken to the next level.

"I don't think we should do anything with them," said Jeremy, "Getting high is just going to put us in danger and make us go through food faster."

"Nothing wrong with having a smoke when we're secure though, is there?" Shawn argued.

"This is a zombie apocalypse! We're never secure!"

"He has a point," Dustin piped up, "Shame we can't sell it to zombies."

"What are you suggesting then? We throw them out?" asked Shawn.

"No... we just leave them..."

"With Robin every evening?" Dustin grinned.

"Robin won't smoke them," said Jeremy, glancing at Robin with uncertainty, "Will you?"

"Nah fam," Robin lied, a sly grin on his face.

"Well what do you think then?"

"I agree with Shawn, we should smoke them," said Robin as though he didn't really care what the outcome of the discussion was.

"Thank you!" Shawn said, beginning his meal of tinned food, "It isn't as if we can use them for anything else."

"True, we should count our blessings on this one," said Dustin, joining them at the table, "I'm sure a lot of survivors would kill to find what we've just found. As long as we only eat at set mealtimes without exception, we should be fine."

There was a brief pause as they all munched out,

before Jeremy broke the silence.

"How are we for food?"

"Ah, this is where we may have a problem," said Dustin glancing nervously at his bag of tins, "At the rate we're going we probably have at most four meals left."

"That including Tommy's stuff?"

"Yep," Dustin nodded, "And we haven't exactly been rationing it either. I know full well that you've all dipped a hand in his biscuit jar. So we're going to need to find some more food. And the sooner the better."

The uncomfortable silence between them all spoke truths. They would have to venture into the outdoor world, which was now a very dangerous thing to do.

"Shit," Jeremy breathed.

"Could be an opportunity to see if any of the Gullum neighborhood is still alive," Shawn pointed out.

"True," Dustin nodded in agreement.

"Wait, I could check to see if my mum is still alive!" Jeremy realized, only just remembering that he had family that lived in Gullum. With all the commotion about survival, the four of them had simply forgotten that they had family. Apart, of course, from Shawn who hoped his brother would be zombified and maybe getting some exercise for once.

Dustin was about to mention that he doubted that Jeremy's mum would still be alive, but he decided against it. It would have been harsh and uncalled for. And potentially inaccurate. His thoughts turned to his own family. They were no doubt unreachable and unlikely to be home. Home being several miles past the Carpathian Mills, a place they had been unable to reach due to zombie hordes. The chances of ever meeting them alive again seemed slim.

And yet he didn't seem to care. Which was what bothered him the most.

The four of them finished their meals, grabbed a melee weapon each and cautiously crept outside. It was time to explore Gullum.

Within the confinements of Tommy's walled garden, they planned their scavenger hunt and plucked up the courage to step out onto the streets. The sun was out in full blazing form, shining down happily upon the dead world.

"Yo, you got that list Robin?" Jeremy held out a hand for the list of supplies they needed that Robin had promised to draw up. It was well detailed:

Food
Water
Weapons
Defenses
FIFA 2013
Fuel
Girls
Anything else important.

"Fifa?" said a clearly unimpressed Dustin, "Seriously? Doesn't Tommy have enough of them?"

"Well fam, y'know, he's missing '13," Robin mumbled, dragging his cricket bat from the ground.

"Thank goodness we don't have power or I'd have to kill myself already," grumbled Dustin.

"Girls?" Jeremy quizzed.

"Yeman, it's a sausagefest here. We need to balance the gender scales the best we can. There's too many man."

"He has a point," replied Shawn as a painful groaning sound floated over Tommy's garden fence, "Just no sketty Gullum fat chicks, we'd be like a burger in too much bread."

They all chuckled nervously. A silence fell between them once again. Nobody wanted to step foot out into the street.

"Sooo then…" Jeremy said, keeping his voice low since zombie activity sounded like it was building up beyond the fence, "How are we gonna do this?"

Dustin flipped the list paper, snatched the pencil off Robin and drew out the street plan of upper Gullum. It mainly consisted of four rows of houses. Each row had its own road, all connecting to Scar Lane which ran down the hill with the rows and continued downwards to lower Gullum. Tommy's house was on the top row. On the other side of Scar Lane, parallel to the second row of houses was the Gullum clock tower. Remembering there was also a blockage on Scar Lane, Dustin shaded in roughly where he thought it was.

"If we focus on these four rows of houses we should be fine," he said.

"So we just have a street each?" Jeremy asked.

"Bad idea, we need to stick together," Dustin replied, "If one of us gets into trouble we'll need support."

"Oh yeah, good point."

"How about we split up in twos then?" Shawn suggested, "Me and Dustin can do the top two rows and you two can do the bottom two."

"Fine by me," said Jeremy, knowing his mother's house was on the bottom row of houses in upper Gullum.

And so it was decided. With care, the four of them slipped out onto the street, immediately attracting the attention of the handful of zombies that were moping about.

"Goddammit!" cursed Dustin as he swung his cricket bat at the face of a zombie, knocking it out of the way and spraying the day's 'first blood' in all directions, "Scar Lane! Quicktime!"

The four of them sprinted down the street towards Scar Lane, swinging out at zombies on the way. Jeremy swung his sword enthusiastically, slicing open a female specimen who continued lumbering after them even when her guts began spilling out upon the tarmac. Both Shawn and Robin were clubbing eager attackers round the head simultaneously, dazing them for a few seconds. Dustin was focused on getting to Scar Lane, and nimbly dodged most of the zombies that were coming at him.

"Later fools!" Shawn joked as he kicked in the door of the house at the end of the street, Dustin pushing away a zombie before catching up.

"Oh shit yea, that's why you wanted to do the first two blocks!" Jeremy realized as Robin checked if Scar Lane was clear.

"No shit!" yelled Dustin, jogging into the house after Shawn, leaving Jeremy and Robin to venture down Scar Lane and search the bottom two rows of houses. Gripping their weapons in anticipation, the pair legged it down the lane, past the Gullum clock tower and to their row of houses.

Like a plague of locusts they quickly stripped the empty houses of their belongings, mostly finding rubbish they didn't want but occasionally finding a better weapon to use or a lone can of food to steal. It seems that most people hadn't been stupid enough to leave their food before fleeing.

Dustin and Shawn found it was easier to break in and out of houses through attic windows rather than the front door and it wasn't long before they saw Jeremy and Robin doing the same.

"Oi! Knob-jockeys!" Dustin yelled across upper Gullum to the two silhouettes upon the roof of the third row of houses as Shawn waved. The silhouettes confirmed they were indeed Jeremy and Robin in the form of several rude gestures.

It was swelteringly hot, or so Dustin thought at least. Rubbing the sweat from his forehead, he glanced down to the street below through the glare of the sun. Zombie activity was still relatively low, nothing close to the carnage they'd narrowly avoided the night previous.

The Gullum clock tower realised it was three o'clock. It celebrated this with three loud chimes, echoing around Gullum and causing the birds in the trees to scatter. A second later, a roar of fury from thousands of zombies. Another second and the streets of Gullum were flooded with a shrieking tsunami of zombies, all racing towards the clock tower and smashing their fists furiously at the structure as though it was the world's most annoying alarm clock that refused to go on snooze. Some had seemingly appeared from nowhere, whilst others had been chewing on corpses and swatting at a poor beanie-wearing man who was stuck up a tree. It was quite a sight as the four of them watched the furious horde pointlessly attack the clock tower.

"I guess that is what we managed to miss last night," said Dustin, noticing that somebody had graffitied the word 'Pesk' several times on the clock tower and wondering what on Earth it was meant to mean.

"True," Shawn replied, "How is the clock tower even working without electricity?"

"Fuck knows. There is probably some old guy still sat in there ringing the bell whenever it needs to ring."

Jeremy and Robin were just as startled by the sight.

"How often does that clock tower go off?" Jeremy asked Robin, "We don't wanna get caught up in all that."

"Dunno fam."

The spectacle continued for about an hour or so and the four of them found themselves breathing a sigh of relief when four o'clock didn't trigger the chimes. Finally, the zombies grew tired of their pointless pursuit and they slowly dwindled away in small groups. Eventually, nearly an hour and a half later, the streets were back to their more calm post-apocalypse state.

During the commotion, Dustin and Shawn had managed to search some houses although they had very little within of use. However their search was cut short due to the lack of attic windows and once the zombie horde had finally died down, they were able to resume their scavenging in the more traditional door-to-door style.

However, this next particular door had a surprise

behind it. Dustin and Shawn found themselves greeted by the wrong end of a shotgun and a rather scruffy middle-aged individual dressed in nothing but boxer shorts and a stained vest.

"One more step and I'll blow ya brains over the pavement," he growled like a pissed off old badger.

Alarmed, Dustin and Shawn backed off, hands hovering in the air slightly.

"Hey, we don't mean any trouble-"

"Bullshit!" he spat in return, his underwear elastic threatening to break under the girth of his large belly, "Ya really think everyone here is dead? I've seen ya raid quite a few houses that people still live in. That's robbery and thievery, sunbeam."

Shawn began to doubt that the shotgun was real after the last few words of his sentence. It was most likely an old man attempting to intimidate them.

"Zombie apocalypse," said Shawn, dropping his hands, "Everything has changed."

"I doubt Duncreek will feel the same when he returns to number twenny-one," said the old man, "But I'll leave that problem with you fellas."

And with that the door was swung closed, slamming loudly and attracting a few zombies.

"Fuck," said Dustin, running to the next house before the zombies caught up to them, "I didn't expect survivors!"

"Neither did I," Shawn breathed.

"How many houses do you think we've raided that people are going to return to?"

"Who gives a fuck? Zombie apocalypse changes everything Dustin. What's he gonna do?"

"Blow our brains over the pavement?"

"Like hell he will. Guns were hard enough to come by before the apocalypse. Now they'll be the rarest thing ever."

"How does that even work? There are no laws now…"

Dustin was confused as he entered the next house, but Shawn never answered. He knew who lived here, although he doubted they had survived. Casper. A ginger gaming friend of theirs.

"Yo Casper!" Dustin called whilst in the kitchen as Shawn stuffed the contents of his fridge into a bag. Certainly their best haul yet, there was enough food in there to last a good few days.

There were sounds of movement from upstairs. Dustin hoped it was Casper, but wasn't taking chances. As Shawn continued his search in the living room, Dustin silently slipped upstairs.

The noise he could here wasn't of human movement. It was a low rumbling, like machinery. Some sort of engine. Making sure his weapon was in a useable position, he burst into Casper's bedroom.

Casper was there. But that probably wasn't the most surprising thing. He was on his PC, playing Rome Total War as though the infestation of zombies had never happened. Strapped to his PC was a generator, rumbling loudly.

"Dustin!" Casper seemed genuinely shocked to see Dustin.

"Fuck you!" Dustin said back at him without even knowing why, "How long have you been held up in here?"

Casper shrugged and continued his roman battle as though it answered his question.

"And you have a generator?" said Dustin in awe, walking over to the noisy machine, "Dude, is this your zombie apocalypse plan? Play Rome until it all blows over?"

"Pretty much."

"It ain't gonna blow over mate, you need to come back with us to Tommy's house."

"You're at Tommy's house?" he replied, still absorbed in his roman battle, "I thought Tommy was on holiday."

"Tommy isn't there. But me, Shawn, Jeremy and Robin

are."

"Speak of the devil and he shall arrive," smiled Shawn as he appeared at the Casper's bedroom door with a bag of his food.

"Is that my food?"

"Yes you wasteman. Coming to Tommy's with us?"

"Looks like I have to now," Casper grumbled, pulling the plug on his PC.

Casper's house did have a lot of useful things. It took them several journeys but they managed to drag back all the food in his house, a laptop, the generator, a can of fuel and several laser pens in varying colours. In predictable style, Casper moaned every step of the way and Dustin was considering that bringing him along hadn't been the best idea.

Jeremy and Robin also returned, also coming back with very little food and not much of great use.

"Is that it?" asked a dumbfounded Dustin when he saw the five measly tins of food they returned with.

"Na fam, we found this at Jeremy's mum's yard," replied Robin, slapping the missing copy of FIFA 2013 in Dustin's hands.

"Oh well, my mind is really at ease now," Dustin quipped sarcastically.

"What the hell are those?" Shawn asked, pointing at the four enclosed curved mirrors that Jeremy had just accidentally dropped in Tommy's garden.

"Carousel mirrors," said a flustered Jeremy, picking them back up, "There's this crashed lorry full of fairground equipment. Thought they'd be useful."

"How?"

Jeremy didn't answer the question.

"Did you find your mum?" Dustin asked.

"Nah, but her body wasn't there so there is still hope," he replied, knowing full well there wasn't any hope at all, "I'd say her dead carcass probably got up and started walking on its own accord."

"A lot of people still living at home isn't there?" commented Robin as he strode past. It seemed they had roughly the same experience as Dustin and Shawn. Lots of occupied houses.

The evening approached quickly. Dustin made them all food again as the rest made post-apocalypse improvements to Tommy's house. Casper busied himself with rigging up the generator to various devices in the house, the radio, the games console, a few lamps and his laptop. Robin entertained himself by picking, bagging up and rolling the weed in Tommy's attic; whilst Shawn and Jeremy continued to improve the houses defenses.

Before they knew it, it was nine o'clock. The Gullum clock tower struck once again as Dustin and Jeremy were both laid out upon Tommy's bed, passing a spliff of Tommy's weed and listening to the radio from downstairs.

"Welcome back Crapital listeners and we have the latest showbiz news for you all right now, before it happens! Britney has shocked us all with her new look today, who'd have known she would take South Park so seriously, but on the plus she has certainly lost a lot of calories. Prad Bitt has been twatted walking around central park with the one arm look, columnists are calling the trend zombification and we are wanting all of your zombified selfies right now-"

"Every three hours," said Jeremy, looking at Dustin as though it was meant to mean something.

"What!?"

"The clock tower!" Jeremy explained, "It goes off every three hours. Twelve, three, six and nine."

"Oh yeah… good point," Dustin replied, blowing out smoke and passing the spliff.

There was a cheer from upstairs as one of either Robin or Shawn had scored a goal on FIFA. Feeling slightly depressed despite the high, Dustin turned to the many more FIFA games and their contradictory slogans piled high on Tommy's shelf. FIFA 2011 – Football Has Changed. FIFA 2012 – Football Never Changes. Fuck FIFA.

"This is crap," Dustin moaned as Jeremy smoked, "Zombie apocalypse. And the only radio station is Crapital. And the only video game is FIFA."

"Heh," chuckled Jeremy, watching the zombies stumble about in the dying light of the outside, "Living Left 4 Dead isn't working out as fun as you thought?"

"It's like living with Fred West."

"True dat," snorted Jeremy as he passed the spliff back to Dustin.

They laid in silence for a moment, absorbing the sounds of the undead stumbling around outside like drunkards, the ignorant voices of Crapital radio drifting from downstairs and the wooden commentary of yet another Red United verses Blue City game; before Dustin broke the silence.

"How long do you think we'll survive?"

Jeremy took a moment of thought before he answered, "It's hard to say. A month tops maybe? Depends how long we can avoid being bitten and how long we manage to find food."

"So you defiantly think we're going to die at some point?"

"Yes," replied Jeremy, "Nobody survives a zombie apocalypse."

"So what you're saying is, this is one circumstance where it will work just like the movies?" Dustin asked, blowing out smoke and passing the spliff.

"Ha. Probably. Why? How long do you think we'll last?"

"No idea. I'm more concerned what other survivors will do to be honest. They'll be struggling for resources just as bad as us."

"I feel ya," Jeremy said, "Me and Robin saw somebody actually driving about today in a Cleo. Fuck knows what they were doing; I think they may have been raiding houses. Didn't you have a gun pulled to your face today?"

"Yeman, but Shawn reckons it wasn't real," said

Dustin, recalling the old man shotgun incident in his mind, "It pranged me out but it did seem odd."

"Yo man, guess who we found today creeping about next door to my mum's?"

"It wasn't Karen Gillan was it?" Dustin asked in hope.

"Nah fam."

"Then I don't give a shit."

"I'm telling you anyway dickhead," Jeremy laughed, passing the spliff back, "It was Moonface."

"Ugh. Moonface? That waste of skin?"

"Yeman."

Moonface was an old friend of theirs, although friend was probably the wrong word. Dustin, Shawn and Jeremy had used Moonface for his free yard and he had used them for their weed. The arrangement began to crumble however when they realized Moonface had all the personality of loaf of stale bread, never actually getting to know them and only caring about his drug supply. Eventually they stopped chilling with him, which prompted him to get into large amounts of debt with his dealer. Since then, they had no clue what happened to him. Other than the endlessly circulating rumors that he'd gotten into several grand's worth of debt with a certain dealer known as 'That Guy.'

"That slippery, spherical, son of a bitch," Dustin spat distastefully, "Of everyone who could survive and it's that loser. What did he have to say for himself?"

Jeremy was just about to answer when Casper yelled something up the stairs.

"Somebody at the door guys! Demanding we let them in! Get down here!"

"Shit."

Somebody arriving was bad news. The last thing they needed either was trouble or an extra mouth to feed. Jumping up, Dustin and Jeremy ran downstairs, Jeremy tripping and almost falling headfirst down the steps as he rushed to find out who had arrived.

"Who is it?" Jeremy demanded, pushing past Casper and his laptop setup in the kitchen.

"Dunno," Casper replied, slight panic in his voice and coughing from the smell of weed, "Calls himself Joshua. Claims he is a friend of Tommy's."

Joshua was stood in the garden looking less than impressed.

"What do you want?" Dustin asked in a harsher tone than he meant.

"This is Tommy's house," sneered Joshua, shrugging as though he had turned up to the wrong bus stop, "Lad told me to meet him here."

"Tommy isn't here," replied Dustin.

"Then where is he?"

"Not here."

"Then why are you here?" Joshua's tone didn't get any friendlier.

"Zombie apocalypse mate," said Jeremy in an unsure voice.

"Yeah, I know but-"

"Where have you even come from?" Dustin asked as Shawn and Robin joined the commotion, their pupils having successfully invaded the rest of their eyes. Quite suddenly, Dustin realized that he was actually very high and too paranoid for a confrontation like this.

"Fortress Mound."

Fortress Mound was a small, decommissioned military fort positioned upon a hill overlooking Morrhead. Dustin knew they had been lucky to make it alive from Coniston the previous day, making it alive from Fortress Mound was an impressive feat.

"Fortress Mound?" repeated a dumbfounded Dustin, not quite sure to believe what he was hearing.

"Yeman. It's trife up there. I wanna go back so I can never go. Standard."

Glancing back at the rest of his group to see if any of them understood what Joshua was talking about, Dustin was unsure what to say. He didn't know what 'trife' was meant to mean or what Joshua wanted.

"So, can I come in? Is Dany here?" he finally asked after a moment of awkwardness.

"No," was the reply off Dustin, Jeremy and Shawn, all at the same time.

"Why not?"

"You could be bit," Jeremy rightfully pointed out.

"So could you."

"But we're not," replied Jeremy.

"Neither am I."

"You can't prove that."

Another awkward silence passed as Joshua weighed up his options, "Well it is Tommy's yard. It's only fair!"

"Ah, no," Dustin said almost immediately, "It's not Tommy's yard anymore. It's ours until he returns."

"How is that even fair?"

"Dunno if you've noticed fam, but it's a zombie apocalypse," Robin piped up from behind Shawn and Jeremy.

"Yeah," continued Shawn, "First come, first serve."

"Don't be west man, let us in!" Joshua was just beginning to realize they were being serious.

"West?" Dustin was confused.

"Yeman. West. Swear down y'all being flids on purpose. Ya got any food?"

"Does this guy speak English?" Dustin heard Casper ask Shawn, who ignored him.

"Look, go find Tommy and come back with him and we'll gladly let you in," said Dustin, getting impatient, "If Tommy is still alive that is."

"Ya chatting breeze mate, taking liberties and all," Joshua replied, looking disgruntled at their rejection, "It doesn't matter if Tommy is alive, it's all relative mate. It's all relative."

Dustin replayed what Joshua had just said in his mind, "It's all relative? What does that even mean?"

"It means you should fucking let me in now and stop chatting breeze mate!" Joshua's behavior took an unexpected aggressive twist, "Tommy ain't gonna be pleased about this!"

"We're not pleased about this either," growled Shawn aggressively, pulling the long sword Jeremy stole from the museum into view as Robin gripped his cricket bat and Jeremy quickly grabbed a spare golf club.

Joshua's angry eyes flickered with defeat upon sight of their weapons.

"Bring it bro if you think you've got it," said Dustin, acutely aware that he didn't have a weapon and was probably the worst out of them all at fighting. Even Casper was probably better.

"Let me in. It's only fair!"

"Life isn't fair," Dustin snapped, beginning to get a little impatient at Joshua's persistence, "Come back with Tommy and we'll talk. Until then, we don't know if you even know him. We don't know if you've been bitten. We don't know what you're up to. We don't know if you're a danger to us. Times are tough."

In a disgruntled manner, Joshua edged himself out of Tommy's small paved garden and into the zombie filled streets that were hidden from view by the large garden fence. The five of them watched the gate momentarily, listening out for Joshua's movements. Once they heard his footsteps of disappointment fade into the distance and merge with the many feet of pacing zombies, they relaxed.

"Did we just send some guy away?" Jeremy asked, clearly feeling guilty.

"Some guy who didn't have a word of sense in him," said Dustin as though Joshua's questionable choice of words settled the matter.

"Yeah, it was the right choice," said Casper, panic no longer in his voice as he returned to his laptop setup in Tommy's kitchen.

"I agree. It was the right choice. Food is tight still," said

Shawn.

"Yeman I'm with Shawn," Robin agreed.

Jeremy still didn't look convinced, so Dustin passed him the spliff to cheer him up.

DAY 3

Robin was first to rise on day three. Like the rest, he was surprised he had survived so long. Laid out on Tommy's camp bed, he almost feared to get up and face the challenges the day would undoubtedly throw at him. He missed his sister, but knew that looking for her would be suicide. This wasn't like in the movies after all.

He glanced across the room at the many cannabis plants chilling in the soft sunlight of the morning that was pouring through the roof window. They smelt damn good, but something was bothering Robin. Standing up, he looked out of the window. As predicted, the zombies were continuing their random strolling through Gullum, although the zombie activity did look quite promisingly low. But that wasn't what was bothering Robin. Something seemed amiss.

It took a few minutes for him to figure it out. It was the silence. Usually the morning was filled with the tweeting of one flock of birds at the very least. Now even the birds were silent. Perhaps they were all dead or left Earth for their true home planet or something. The lack of wildlife was unnerving and as his shaky hands pulled the sticky bud straight from the stalk for the first spliff of the day, Robin found himself wondering if animals could be turned into zombies too or if it was just a human only affair.

Dustin made breakfast once again. The gas was no longer functional so his role of 'making' it was reduced to grabbing each of them a fork and opening a tin of food.

"I don't want chicken soup, can't I have a full English?" Jeremy moaned, looking at his open can with dismay.

"Whatever," Dustin said, swapping it with his full English in a tin.

"Casper, you seriously having rice pudding for breakfast?" Shawn asked.

"I like it," was the reply Shawn got. Casper didn't even look up.

"How was sleeping on the sofa?"

"Lumpy."

They ate in silence for a while. None of them were in the mood to chat.

"Ugh, I don't like mushrooms, swap back?" Jeremy continued, determined to whine about something, his eyes looking at an object on the end of his fork that may or may not have been a mushroom.

"Fuck off," Dustin replied.

The awkward silence continued, only the sound of Casper's moist chomping as he wolfed his tin of rice pudding was hitting against their eardrums. The mood and atmosphere was at an all-time low. Reality had hit them all. Surviving was no longer a joke. They would have to take it seriously if they actually wanted to succeed.

"Yo," Jeremy gasped for breaths between eating and speaking, "How much food do we even have here? A week's worth?"

Nobody knew.

"Yeah, we need to decide how we're going to do this," said Dustin, throwing his empty can upon the table, which clattered loudly.

"What you mean?" Robin asked, the large pupils in his eyes clearly giving away what he spent the night doing in Tommy's attic.

"At this rate we're going to die. We need a solid plan. We're all over the place like a mad woman's shit. Anyone with any ideas?"

Dustin's question was met with silence and the sound of crunching tobacco as Jeremy rolled himself a cigarette.

"Anything?"

"We could try besieging their province capital, make sure you have at least two battering rams and a couple of ladders. Flaming pigs will help against the elephants. Keep the pressure on the gates and send a few units round the back to sandwich them in-"

"We're not playing Rome Total War Casper," said Jeremy, "And anyway, that's a retarded tactic. Using siege equipment is the wrong way to go about taking a province capital."

"What's wrong with scavenging?" Shawn asked.

"Other than the fact that last time we found nothing but trouble and an extra mouth to feed?"

"Good point. You thinking we move onto the Carpathian Mills?"

"No, that's equally as retarded," said Dustin, "And if it is anything like Gullum most of the residents will probably be just continuing as normal it seems, meaning there will be nothing to scavenge. It's worth a try, but we can't expect anything of it. And moving there for good would be a huge risk."

"I am surprised how many people are still alive here," said Shawn.

"Me too," said Jeremy, "Shame we're sat on their old bud supply, ha!"

Jeremy's comment was met with silence was cog whirred in their heads.

"Could it really be that simple?" asked Dustin to nobody since nobody had a clue as to what he was on about.

"What?"

"We could continue what Tommy was doing before this whole zombie apocalypse."

"What? Deal drugs?" Robin asked.

"Exactly," continued Dustin, "We have everything we need. We have plants, seeds, bags, books on how to grow the stuff-"

"-papers, blunts, bongs-"

"-all the ingredients for a high... um... pie."

"Now that is a retarded idea," said Casper, clearly unimpressed.

"Well let's hear your amazing idea then Casper," said Shawn. All eyes were now upon Casper.

"I don't have one!" Casper snapped at them, "But at least I'm not considering breaking the law!"

"Um... there is no law Casper," Jeremy pointed out.

"Yeah, zombie apocalypse, remember? Everything's changed."

"I still don't like it," grumbled a defiant Casper.

"It's an avenue worth exploring," insisted a definite Dustin, "I just hope there is still demand for weed in Gullum."

"Well it is Gullum after all," Robin pointed out, "We'd probably sell out easy."

"This is stupid."

"What do you suggest we do then Casper?" asked Shawn once again.

"Yeman, we're all fucking ears!" snapped Dustin, getting irritated at Casper's constant lack of faith.

Casper floundered. He had no ideas and it was obvious.

"How about we vote on it? Majority rules," Dustin suggested, "All in favour of continuing Tommy's legacy, flip Casper off."

Casper found himself staring at four middle fingers. He was outvoted four to one. In a disgruntled manner, he sulked off to his laptop, which had been relying off battery power all morning.

"So then? How are we going to do this?"

That was the big question. And over the course of the morning the four of them discussed ways to make the idea work as Casper moaned at them and his game of Rome Total War. Their discussions took several hours, debating and planning all the logistics required for such a risky idea. Ideas were discussed, argued over and often thrown metaphorically out of the window as time passed. It was past midday before they arrived at something that looked like a workable and feasible plan.

"So just to recap," said Dustin, staring at the pad of hastily scribbled ideas they had spent the morning forming, "We're limiting this trial to Upper Gullum, sectioning it into four parts, streets A to D. We pin an advert flier on street C, saying we're selling draws of bud in exchange for two tins of food-"

"-I still think that's too high," interrupted Shawn.

"-maybe it is, we'll soon find out," Dustin replied before continuing, "Anyway, draws of bud in exchange for two tins and that if anybody is interested they have to sign below. If we have signatures tomorrow morning, we take the flier, sort out the orders and meet our clients on street C once again as the clock tower distracts the zombies away at six.

"If it all works out, we can make our assigned roles permanent. The roles being as follows. Myself, growing and quality assurance. Jeremy, promotion and sales. Shawn, security. Robin, delivering-"

"We never thought of a thing for Casper to do," Jeremy interrupted.

"I've told you I want no part of this!" Casper's voice floated from behind Robin along with the sound of roman units slaughtering barbarians.

"Tough shit yo!" said Shawn in a raised voice, slowly turning to face Casper in a slightly menacing way, "This is what we've decided and you're either helping us or you can fuck off!"

"You were the ones who insisted I come with you!" Casper protested, "You're using my generator! Why should I help you?"

"Because you're outnumbered four to one?" suggested Dustin.

"Yo, you can't be seriously suggesting we kick him out?" scowled Jeremy, "I know he's a wasteman but he's our friend."

"Zombie apocalypse brah."

"If he isn't any use, then what is the point in him? This is serious stuff and he's treating it like a joke!"

"I'm treating it like a joke!?" Casper paused his game, showing a face full of annoyance, "I'm not the one who is suggesting that dealing illegal drugs is a good idea to survive the zombie apocalypse."

"Then what do you suggest? Let me guess, 'I don't know,'" Shawn mocked just as Casper protested that he didn't know what they should do.

"Let's face it Casper, this weed of Tommy's is the only resource we have," said Dustin, trying to convince him, "We'd be foolish not to try and trade it. And if it works out, there is no reason why we can't grow some more. We easily have two years' worth of seeds up there, perhaps more."

All eyes were upon Robin who had yet to comment on Casper's lack of confidence in their plan.

"What?" he asked when he noticed four pairs of eyes staring at him, "I agree with Shawn, whatever."

"You always agree with Shawn," Casper moaned.

"Agreed," said Jeremy, "Anyway, even if Casper was willing to help out, what could he do exactly? He can't fight, he refuses to touch drugs and he is the most stubborn person I've met-"

"-I am still here you know," said Casper, annoyance in his voice as Robin began toying around with one of the laser pens out of boredom.

"Fuck off, I'm sticking up for ya!" Jeremy snapped.

Dustin realised that Jeremy had a good point. What could they get Casper to do? He glanced at their scribbled plan as the other four hurled themselves into an argument. They had a grower, a deliverer, a promotions guy and someone to ensure security. What else did they need? As Dustin racked his brains the heated debate before him blurred into the background of his senses. What else did they need? What was Casper good at?

The answer hit him so hard he found it impossible to think that any of them had not thought it before.

"Yo, yo!" Dustin called above the argument at the risk of being so loud he'd attract the zombies from outside, "Spreadsheets!"

"Wot?"

"Casper can be the guy who is in charge of spreadsheets," Dustin explained, "He has a craptop and he is undeniably good at them. He can act as the accountant, managing our resources, pulling up useful statistics for us to work on and making sure there aren't ever any discrepancies or missing stock."

"Yo, so basically you propose to put Casper pretty much in charge," Shawn asked, clearly unimpressed.

"Yeah," Dustin nodded, "Just of resource management."

There was a nasty silence.

"I'll do it!" Casper had instantly changed his tune, a huge grin on his face as he turned back to his laptop and eagerly waited for Excel to load.

Shawn didn't look happy, "This doesn't put you fully in charge you know. We still have an equal vote each of what occurs."

"Yeah!" Robin agreed, still flashing the laser pen around the room.

"All in favour of making Casper our resources accountant, put your hands up."

The vote was reluctantly unanimous. Everyone agreed to Dustin's idea. Casper was the accountant.

"There you go Casper," smiled Dustin, "Enjoy your authoritah. You better be bloody good at this."

"Oh, don't you worry," grimaced Casper, as everyone slowly got up from the table, "I'm already in the Lotus position. It's even going to have charts."

"Make sure it's done for when we've finished setting up," Dustin continued, "We need solid stats!"

"You never finish a spreadsheet. You just stop working on it," was the reply they all got from a Casper who had his head two oxygen atoms away from his laptop screen as he frantically hammered at the keyboard as though he was attempting to get a high score on whack-a-mole.

"What now?" asked Jeremy. They were all stood up for no apparent reason.

"Scavenge some more? Whilst me and Dustin sort out a communication system for Robin when he's out delivering?" Shawn suggested.

"Fine, me 'n' Jeremy will check out lower Gullum then innit," said Robin, still looking high as he dropped the laser pen in favour of Tommy's cricket bat.

Jeremy and Robin silently slipped out of Tommy's front door and into the infected but pleasantly sunny world outside.

"A communication system for Robin?" Dustin questioned over the sound of Casper's fingers ablaze on the keyboard, "Way to set us the impossible job Shawn."

"Couldn't be farced with scavenging," said a grumpy sounding Shawn as he slouched back down at the kitchen table and began poking at the laser pen Robin left behind.

"True talk," Dustin agreed, remembering their disastrous attempts at gathering resources, "If today is anything like yesterday them guys will come back with a load of junk we don't need and another lucky wanker with a generator."

Other than the constant pitter-patter of keyboard keys being struck by Casper, the house was silent as a mausoleum. Dustin glanced around idly. They had certainly acquired a lot of junk. Potentially useful junk, but still junk. Broken furniture, useless electronic devices, the weird carousel mirrors that Jeremy brought back and piles of CDs, books and DVDs all cluttered the kitchen. Within it all he spotted a copy of Lord of the Bongs and was tempted to give it a read when Shawn spoke again.

"We need walkie talkies obviously," he said, not showing much enthusiasm for their task.

"We don't have any," replied Casper, checking his partially completed spreadsheet.

"Mister formula here has it all worked out already," Dustin said, partially impressed that Casper was managing their resources so fast.

"Don't joke just yet," Casper warned as he typed busily away, "It's easy to make mistakes using formulas. But if you really want to foul things up, write a macro."

"How many lame spreadsheet jokes do you know Casper?" asked Dustin, looking unimpressed at Casper's effort at humour.

"I excel at humourless jokes," Casper protested, "I have the formula down to a tee."

"Yeah, well, any more like that and I'll put you in a cell."

Shawn ignored Casper's failed attempts at mathematical wit and continued to mentally wrack his mind for a way to communicate.

A few minutes of keystroke-filled silence followed once more as neither of them managed to muster a solution. Dustin's mind was attempting to mentally combine every item they had stashed with one another as though he was trying to solve a puzzle in a point and click adventure game. His mind drew a blank. Shawn had gone and set them an impossible task.

Dustin hashed together something that resembled a

plan, however was actually a way to get rid of FIFA in disguise, "Uh… we could use the FIFA discs to reflect sunlight above the houses…"

"That's just a way to get rid of FIFA in disguise isn't it?" Shawn replied, seeing straight through Dustin's words, "We may as well use them mirror things and Casper's laser pens if we're using light."

They glanced down at the set of carousel mirrors that Robin and Jeremy had returned with the previous day. They were both curved, maybe good enough to be placed on the roofs of houses and used to shine laser pen light down for communication across Gullum.

And that is how Dustin and Shawn found themselves upon the roofs of two different houses in the sweltering Gullum sunshine. Gullum itself was mostly quiet, the zombie population barely brushing double figures as the unusually powerful sun that was basking the rows of houses. Dustin and Shawn had flipped a coin to decide who would have to go a couple of blocks down the road. To his dismay, Dustin had lost the cushy option. There were however, worse days to lose and with the zombie activity at an all-time low, he found his journey two blocks down a cakewalk.

Now they were attempting to align the two carousel mirrors directly opposite each other.

"This idea is kinda shit actually!" Shawn called as he shone the laser pen through the mirror to check they were in the right position for the light to bounce to Dustin's carousel mirror. The laser light missed Dustin's mirror by a few inches, shining eternally into the distance towards Morrhead centre.

"It's the best we can do!" Dustin replied, squinting at Shawn's silhouette through the blinding sunlight that was facing him, "And there is no reason why it shouldn't work."

"You need to budge up right a little!"

Dustin moved to his right, dragging the mirrors with

him along the roof tiles.

"Noo! My right ya poomplex!"

Dustin moved to his left. Shawn's laser light struck Dustin's mirror and was bounced down onto the road below. All that was left for them to do was to place the remaining two carousel mirrors upon the ground, one on what they were calling 'Street C' and one on 'Street A' where Tommy's house was situated. Shawn and himself were able to successfully flash laser pens at each other, two streets apart. Once Dustin pinned up an advertisement, the mission was accomplished.

Got food but need food? The I Shower Naked Club are your dudes. Two tins of food for a draw of sticky peng peng. Sign below and return here at 5:45pm tomorrow with payment.

"What are we saying?" asked Dustin he had returned to Tommy's house, three different colours of laser pen in his hand.

"Well, green for go, so if the deals are all good to go through with we can bring the required amount of bud down," Shawn began, "Amber for no, so if they don't have enough to pay us we don't send the bud down. And red for alert or something for if Robin is being attacked."

"So we're not actually letting Robin have the bud?"

"Not until we know people are going to pay us what we've asked. We don't want any wastemen pulling wastemen stunts."

"True dat."

With a very basic method of communication hashed out, Dustin and Shawn joined Casper with cataloguing their inventory until Jeremy and Robin returned.

"Sup bitches," breathed Jeremy as he dropped a couple bags of tins and slumped on a kitchen chair as though he'd just spent a hectic afternoon Christmas shopping as Robin followed him in with every copy of FIFA that lower Gullum possessed.

"Seriously? More FIFA?" Dustin protested, "What the fuck was the point in getting all that shit? We need food and useful stuff! Not every version of a shitty football game that has been exactly the same since it was first conceived!"

"Yeman, why didn't you guys raid the corner shop?" Shawn asked, frowning.

"Because somebody thought of that yesterday," Robin replied, stacking the back catalogue of FIFA down with the rest.

"It looked like a bomb had gone off in it," Jeremy added over the sound of Casper's keystrokes, "Not even a Cornetto left. How's the communication thing gone?"

Shawn beckoned Jeremy and Robin to follow him outside and showed off the laser pen reflecting system they had set up.

"So they were useful after all," said Jeremy somewhat triumphantly, noticing the use of the carousel mirrors he had found.

With the evening approaching fast, promising only darkness and some zombie attracting bells, Dustin once again took it upon himself to make a meal for them all. With the extra tins Jeremy and Robin had found, they had roughly a weeks-worth of food, if they rationed just right. However, at the meal table, Casper had his own issues.

"We're fine for food and weed, for now at least," he said, wolfing through his cold tin of spaghetti alphabet, "We're not good for generator fuel. You need to find more."

"What kind of fuel is it?" Dustin asked.

"Diesel I think."

"We'll have to rob a fuel station then," said Shawn, not even looking up from a piece of paper he was scribbling delivering plans on.

"There is a Jet on Morrhead Road that isn't too far away," Jeremy suggested, "All we have to do is slip down into Lower Gullum and we're pretty much there innit."

"How desperate are we for fuel?" Dustin asked, noticing both the generator and Casper's laptop were powered off, "How many hours of power do we have left?"

Casper glanced at the generator and had a split second of thought, "If you're wanting to play FIFA tonight, we need some."

"Heh, just as well, fuck FIFA," replied Dustin.

"Yo, fuck you," Shawn piped up.

"Yeah fuck you," Casper retorted, "I have an important appointment with Total War this evening. Rome will fall! Rome has to fall!"

"Crapital FM's chart show is on too innit," Robin piped up as though that too was a justifiable excuse to risk arse to get some fuel.

"Fine, fine!" Dustin scowled, "But we can't go to the Jet! That's stupid. It'll have been raided already."

"Okay then, we need a fuel station that nobody knows about then," said Casper as the Gullum bells outside chimed six.

"There are no other fuel stations around here!" Jeremy protested, "Not unless we're going all the way back to Morrhead centre!"

"Isn't there one in Sinthwaite?" Shawn asked Dustin.

"Yeah, but its even further away than the Carpathian Mills and it'll probably have been the first fuel station to get raided."

"Yo, there's gotta be summat we can use as fuel!" Jeremy vented.

The way Jeremy said that statement made Dustin wonder. Not where they can find fuel, but what they can use as fuel. Something clicked in his head.

"Chip fat oil," he said to an oblivious group.

"Eh?"

"Spent oil used to cook chips, that can run this generator can't it?"

"I think so," said Casper, glancing at the currently

silent generator.

"The restaurant in the Carpathian Mills would save it in barrels round the back because they were cheapskates and didn't want to pay for it to be disposed," explained Dustin, "There's probably at least thirty barrels hidden around there."

"How do you know this?" Casper asked in a pointlessly accusing manner.

"Because I used to work there dumb shit," Dustin snapped back, not even sure why Casper felt the need to ask that, "Anyway, we can kill two birds with one stone. Canal it over there, get the fuel, have a poke around the mills and be back before anybody notices."

The plan sounded simple enough and at roughly seven in the evening, they were all set for an adventure to Sinthwaite. Well, nearly all of them. Casper had taken it upon himself to courageously stay behind and guard Tommy's house whilst they were away.

Zombie activity had increased. And Robin had apparently written another list.

Food
Water
Weapons
Defenses
FIFA ~~2013~~ *2003*
Fuel
Girls
Anything else important.

"That's the same list as before," Jeremy stated the obvious.

"Still gets the job done," was Robin's answer.

Together, they snuck out of Gullum and towards the canal towpath that took them straight to the Carpathian Mills. It was a clear night, the stars in the sky looking down upon the desolate world, twinkling sympathetically to them from a billion light-years away. The four of them hurried along the towpath, as silently as they could, attempting to attract as little attention as possible as the cool night air gently washed over them.

Within ten minutes the Carpathian Mills were in sight. It was a large rectangular structure, five floors high, stood proudly overlooking the canal. Usually, the place was lit up by the many apartments, spa and restaurant held within like some huge oblong Christmas tree. With the lack of electricity and general zombie apocalypse events however, the mill was shrouded in a gloomy darkness. The only source of light was a single car that appeared to have its interior lights on, the rest of the cars sat in the car park either burnt out or broken beyond repair.

"Do you know where to go?" someone asked as they approached the building via the car park. A small handful of zombies were milling around in the twilight, not really paying much attention to anything but the burnt out car they surrounded.

"Of course I do," Dustin replied quietly, getting a little sick of dumb questions, "Me and Shawn will find the oil we need, you guys just forage the hell out of the place. We'll meet back on the canal in thirty."

"Sure thing," replied Jeremy, griping his cricket bat with enthusiasm, "Just one thing first. How the fuck do we get in!?"

"The door," Dustin pointed at a door shaped hole in the wall that probably once contained a door.

"Oh ye," feeling slightly foolish, Jeremy dived into the darkness followed by Robin.

With Jeremy and Robin occupied, Dustin lead Shawn round the back of the mills. In the darkness of a small courtyard, he fumbled for a latch on a length of rope that was securing a large piece of tarpaulin down over something. Within minutes he had pulled the tarpaulin off and revealed ten blue barrels.

"One each or just one?" Shawn asked as Dustin

pushed one of the barrels on its side to roll. Unfortunately for him the lid popped off and oil sloshed out of the barrel in the darkness.

"Oops!" said Dustin, jumping out of the way of the spillage, "I think one should do it. I doubt this stuff is going anywhere if we do run out."

"Well in that case I'll do it this time," said Shawn, turning another barrel to its side with care as Dustin secured the tarpaulin over the rest of the barrels.

As he ensured the tarpaulin was definitely not going to be caught by the blustery Morrhead winds, something occurring within the Mills caught his eye. A flashing light on the fourth floor, blinking silently in the darkness as Shawn casually kicked away a crawler that had followed them and decided to bathe in the pool of oil.

"Yo, you see that?" Dustin asked, pointing at the where the flashing had occurred. Shawn looked to see nothing but darkness.

"What?"

"There was something-"

"There's nothing."

"But there was something-"

"Whatever Dustin," Shawn turned and rolled the barrel of oil towards the car park.

Dustin paused and continued stared at the Mills some more, somewhat perplexed. Nothing flashed at him again so he followed Shawn around to the car park.

The car park continued to be silent as Shawn rolled the barrel and Dustin followed closely behind. The zombies were still distracted with the car wreckage. Things appeared to be calm.

"Look! There it is again!" Dustin hissed, pointing up at the fourth floor. Shawn looked. Sure enough, there was a bright white light flashing from within.

"It could be just Robin or Jeremy."

"They don't have torches! We should check it out."

"And what? Have another mouth to feed? You said

yourself that it's the last thing we need!"

Dustin paused and glanced back up at the flashing, "Look, how about we just check it out? I'm curious and we have another quarter of an hour before we're due to meet them."

"And what about the oil?"

"Just leave it here, if someone robs it we can quickly grab another."

With an exasperated sigh, Shawn rolled the barrel to the side of the mill and followed Dustin into the darkness of the building.

Meanwhile, Jeremy and Robin were not having a fun time. They had made their way to the third floor, fumbling around in the sheer darkness, and found nothing much of interest. The apartments that the mill contained were mostly trashed and blood-soaked. As he stepped over some poor soul's innards that were scattered down the third floor corridor, Jeremy couldn't help thinking that serious shit went down in the building the day the apocalypse occurred.

"Yo fam, this is pathetic, FIFA isn't anywhere in sight!" Robin whispered without even knowing why he was whispering.

"This way," Jeremy ushered Robin into an apartment to their right that looked to have considerably less blood on the broken door than the rest.

Unlike the rest of the apartments, this one appeared mostly untouched. Jeremy scanned the room, taking in all that was there. Television, DVD player, hair straighteners, cheap tablet, discarded nail files, several broken phone chargers, Zomb Direction poster, several DVDs scattered about that all looked like romantic comedies and an entire shelf of make-up stuff that may as well have been highly advanced alien technology for all they knew. No sight of anything useful.

"Hey!" Robin whispered, pointing up the apartment's stairs. There was a flashing light somewhere upstairs. It wasn't a soft pulse of a sleeping electronic device, it was a jarring and constant on-off-on-off. Until it stopped that is, and captured the curiosity of Jeremy and Robin's minds.

With caution the pair found themselves creeping up the stairs fearfully towards what they dearly hoped was going to be a malfunctioning light bulb.

As Jeremy turned the corner up the flight of stairs, the flashing began again, illuminating the word 'pesk' that somebody had daubed on the wall.

Something above creaked.

Someone was up there.

Stifling his breath, Jeremy slipped up the remaining stairs with Robin close behind him.

A silhouette became instantly visible as soon as he turned the landing. With a roar, Jeremy rushed the figure with his weapon as the figure did exactly the same. Two golf clubs clashed against each other as Jeremy found himself face to face with Dustin.

"You!" Dustin hissed, lowering his weapon.

"Yo! Don't scare me like that!" Jeremy exhaled, narrowly avoiding clubbing Robin over the head as he carelessly lowered his golf club, "I thought you were with Shawn."

"He is," Shawn appeared from the apartment bedroom.

"What!? What about the oil-"

"Don't worry about that, it's sorted. Something was flashing in here that's why we came up," said Dustin, looking about in the landing's darkness, "It wasn't you guys was it?"

"Nah fam, we were following that too," Robin replied.

"So where is it then?"

As if it was waiting for that very line as a cue, the flashing began again. It came from within the bathroom, a closed door to the side of Dustin and Jeremy. In silence, the flashing continued, illuminating and plunging them into darkness repetitively until it stopped about half a minute later.

Everyone else hesitated and with his patience wearing thin, Dustin swung the door open. And then immediately wished he hadn't.

The open door and the malfunctioning bathroom light revealed a blood soaked bathroom where nightmares were made. Body parts, both insides and outsides were scattered about the place. In the sink was what looked like a pair of kidneys, the toilet was gurgling and the bath was filled to the brim with the dirtiest looking blood Dustin had seen. But that wasn't the worst bit.

Strapped to a grimy radiator on the wall was a woman. Dustin found it hard to determine an age due to that she appeared to be cobbled together from several body parts. Both arms and legs were certainly not her own and some horrible scarring on her torso probably meant that neither were several of her internal organs. But none of that was the worst bit.

She was still alive. Pleading eyes stared at Dustin through the blinking light as sown up lips hummed and bubbled with high-pitched desperation.

"Oh fuck!"

"That's sick," Jeremy pulled a face of disgust.

"At least we can tick girls off the list now-" Robin began.

Without even allowing a moment of thought to fully take in what they had just seen and before Robin decided to come up with any more inappropriate jokes, Dustin had the bathroom door slammed shut.

"Let's go," he said, walking away.

"Wait, yo, she needs our help!" Robin protested.

"Yeah, seriously Dustin? Are we really just going to leave her there?" Shawn asked.

Dustin sighed, "Are we really going to get involved in this?"

"Wouldn't you want to be helped?"

"She's beyond help," Dustin replied defiantly, "She's fucking Frankenstein's monster. Let's get out of here and forget all this ever happened."

"Least we can do is put her out of her misery," said Jeremy. Shawn nodded with agreement and Robin crossed an item out on his list.

Three faces stared at Dustin.

"What are you looking at me for? If you're gonna kill her, do it goddammit!"

Jeremy slowly and unwillingly re-opened the bathroom door. The repugnant sight hit their eyes once more.

"Actually... fuck that," Jeremy's eyes looked like they were about to pop out from his skull.

They were all just about to take the coward's way out and walk away, when the woman began screaming, her lips torn away by the stitching that was keeping her mouth closed. It was a stomach wrenching sight as the four of them stared at the woman scream and writhe in pain, her mouth now nothing but a torn and bloody mess.

Her scream was probably the most alarming thing of all. It was really loud, deafening in fact. Robin doubled over and smothered his ears with his hands. Dustin felt his vision literally blur due to the noise as he followed suit and covered his ears.

A silence followed as the woman gulped down mouthfuls of air in her agonised state. It didn't last long. There was a horrible sound of screaming fury off Sinthwaite's zombies. They had been caught. If there were ever such a thing as being caught by zombies.

"Right," Dustin said decisively, indicating enough was enough, "We are leaving. Quicktime!"

Totally forgetting about the doomed woman, the four of them leaped down the stairs and out of the apartment. Shawn immediately shoved the cricket bat he was holding into the face of an oncoming zombie that was flailing down the corridor at mass speed towards them. The zombie was knocked back at equal speed, allowing them all access through to the emergency stairs.

As they spiralled down with urgency, Dustin saw a colossal swarm of zombie-like shadows flood in and occupy the car park through the staircase windows. Their shadows contorted far along the tarmac in the little light the night provided. The situation was starting to look grim.

Bursting out of the emergency doors they scanned the darkness of the car park. The zombies of Sinthwaite seemed furious their slumber had been interrupted by the scream of a woman. Or they were ravenous and needed to feed. Either way, they were flooding into the car park un-relentlessly from every direction. If the four of them didn't act now, they would be torn to pieces within seconds.

Shawn kicked over the barrel of oil and sent it rolling towards the oncoming horde of zombies. Whatever his plan was, it failed. Instead of the zombies toppling like bowling alley pins, the barrel simply bounced back off them, landing at Shawn's feet once again.

"Yo, over here!" yelled Jeremy, pointing towards an illuminated car with an open door. It was a risk, requiring them to battle through the oncoming horde, but the only solution at the time. Shawn kicked the barrel once again as the four of them charged towards the zombies and the car.

Through the dual powers of sheer luck and hitting zombies, the four of them made it to the car unscathed. Many of the zombies seemed more interested in the Carpathian Mill itself rather than the four of them escorting oil. They managed to make it into the car with the oil before the main bulk of the horde managed to arrive.

"Shit son! The keys are still here!" said Dustin with surprise once they had all gotten safely in, the barrel of oil nestling between Jeremy and Shawn in the back seats.

"No shit," said an unsurprised Robin, "That's why the lights were on."

Feeling their escape has been perhaps a little too easy,

Dustin turned the key and had the car splutter to a start. His thoughts had been right. It had been too easy.

"GOOD EVENING MORRHEAD! TODAY IS THE THIRD DAY OF THE ZOMBIFICATION TREND AND IT IS SAFE TO SAY IT IS STILL THE HOTTEST THING ON TWATTER RIGHT NOW! NEVER BEFORE HAVE WE SEEN SUCH A TREND TAKE HOLD OF THE WORLD LIKE THIS-"

"Shit, shit, shit!" Dustin struggled helplessly with the radio controls as the obnoxious sound of Crapital FM blared out to the citizens of Sinthwaite. The zombies began to take more notice of them and within moments the car was surrounded.

"-SO LET'S TAKE A LOOK AT THE LATEST TWATS! BETH FROM SUNDERLAND SAYS THAT 'OMG I'M SO JELLY OF ANGELINA'S LEGLESS LOOK THAT I'M GOING OUT RIGHT NOW TO BE BITTEN AND HAVE MY LEGS CHOPPED OFF!' YOU GO GIRL! THIS TREND NEEDS LEGS TO CONTINUE AND EVERY-BODIES SUPPORT HAS BEEN INCREDIBLE-"

"Drive!" yelled Shawn as the car was rocked from side to side and a zombie arm crashed through Jeremy's window and attempted a swipe at his kidneys.

Dustin stamped on the accelerator and the car screeched over the zombies in front of them. Keeping his foot down, Dustin swerved on two wheels to avoid a tree, taking out a few more zombies on the way as the radio continued to scream at them about Twatter trends. Missing the car park entrance and crashing straight through the surrounding wooden fence, Dustin span the car round in a circle accidentally as the zombies continued to chase them. Ignoring the smoke gushing from the bonnet, he forced the spluttering car to press onwards towards Gullum.

"Yo! Keep it steady Dustin! Robin's skinning up!"

DAY 4

It was another still morning as Shawn walked through Gullum. Their fourth day. He was surprised they had all managed to survive the events thrown at them so far and was starting to believe that they were possibly infallible. Their escape from the Carpathian Mills had been sheer luck. If that car hadn't been there to aid them, they'd probably be dead.

The zombie count was conveniently low once more. Their car chase from Sinthwaite the previous night had dragged a lot of Sinthwaite zombies over to Gullum. However, once they had crashed the car into the back of the bus they had previously crashed and hidden well behind the defences of Tommy's house, the zombies ploughed onwards towards Morrhead City centre. By the time the following morning had arrived, the deadly horde had moved onwards.

Shawn had good news for the gang. He had been to check their advertisement they had pinned up on Street C and was genuinely surprised with what he saw.

"We have orders!" was the first thing he said when he entered Tommy's house, throwing a copy of their orders down upon the kitchen table.

"Fuck off," Casper replied, was still having trouble believing that the four of them had managed to successfully find some fuel for his generators at the Carpathian Mills, "It has to be a joke."

Dustin, Jeremy and Robin gathered round the order sheet. It wasn't a joke. There were six orders.

Name	Draws
Rouse	1
Rudderman	9
Moonface	1
Kristoff	4
Boltz	2
Christian	1

"Shit son!" Jeremy exclaimed, "That's two... six... seven... eleven... twelve thirteen draws!"

"Sorted, I guess that means we're in business!"

Thirteen draws meant twenty six tins of food. Without a doubt a decent first haul. If everyone was indeed serious about their order.

"Heh, even Moonface wants a draw," Dustin commented.

"He better have the payment, I know what that loser is like," said Jeremy.

"Bet they're all dead by now," Casper drawled, as optimistic as ever.

"I bet you'd be dead if we hadn't found you," Dustin replied shortly.

"My barbarian army would be dead for sure."

"Shut the fuck up you fucking claptrap!"

"I still think two tins is too much to ask for a draw," Shawn piped up, "I think we could have had more orders if we just charged one tin."

"The whole idea is stupid!" Casper added.

"Yo, we already know you hate the idea Casper," Jeremy retorted, "And two tins isn't enough for what we're offering."

"Herp derp two tins is fine!" Dustin debated back impatiently, "Listen right, we technically have a monopoly. Nobody else round here is doing this. We need to make as much as we can whilst that remains. Two tins is a fair price for what we're giving."

"Y'all mad I swear it."

"Fuck you Casper."

Tensions were high. With Casper's strong opposition their plans, the food supplies rapidly dwindling, and having had all of the recent horrible experiences they had lived though so far, there was a disheartened and pessimistic mood overall. It hadn't been the first time they had snapped at one another that morning.

However, with the news of interest in their post-apocalyptic business, spirits were raised a little. Even if Casper was right and all of their clients were indeed now dead.

Dustin set about taking his quality control role in a serious manner, making sure he had thirteen draws prepared for quarter to six. A somewhat peaceful afternoon passed with only noise made from the un-dead outside and Casper moaning about post-apocalyptic life in general in-between his long sessions of fighting off Roman legions on his video game.

Both Shawn and Robin had spent the slowly passing time reading one of Tommy's books, Fifty Shades of Green whilst Jeremy preoccupied himself with building additional defences around Tommy's garden. The zombies had been busy as they passed overnight, tearing down some parts of their fence. It was nothing devastating, but Jeremy was in the mood for building and smacking the heads off the zombies that got too close. It was surprising how soft dead flesh was.

"Yo fam," Shawn mumbled, glancing up from the amazing-ness of the book he was reading, "This whole zombie apocalypse thing was exciting at first but now it's getting like Eastenders. Just with zombies in the background."

"Who are you speaking to?" Casper's grating voice floated from behind a laptop.

"Nobody in particular," was the reply he got.

"It ain't like Eastenders blud," Jeremy said from outside, "No drama innit."

"True, true. We need somebody to have an affair or piss someone off or something," Robin said quietly without taking his eyes from the book.

Shawn strolled along Street C once again, pushing an empty shopping trolley that had been stolen from Didl. Zombie activity was still low. Street C had a total of three roaming about aimlessly, one of which had no legs, and left a trail of black blood wherever it dragged itself. The sun had already set, however it wasn't fully dark yet. Morrhead City gleamed at him in the dying twilight as he breathed the crisp summer air and waited for the buyers. Meanwhile, back at Tommy's house, Robin was waiting with the perfectly prepared draws Dustin had sorted. All he had to do was wait for the all clear and head down with the gear.

Three minutes to go. Gullum was a tranquil and quiet.

Casper was still using the Carpathian oil to fuel his quest for world domination under the name of Rome. Dustin and Jeremy were sat close by, wondering if Casper would ever return to reality and waiting for Shawn's signal.

Two minutes to go. Shawn began to see people approach from the end of the street. They were armed with various makeshift weapons for use against the zombies. He saw Moonface take a swing at one of the oblivious zombies milling around. The zombie collapsed. It looked like the deal was about to go ahead.

A minute later and Shawn was surrounded by the potheads of Gullum. A tall guy with a short raggedy beard and small square glasses. Another tall blonde dude who was dressed in nothing but shorts, t-shirt and flip-flops.

Another blonde, much smaller with vivid blue eyes, looked a bit Nazi-like. A guy who looked like he had dressed for winter, glassy eyes peeking from under a mammoth of a woolly hat. Next to him was a short dumpy guy, again, blonde hair, but looked much tougher than the other two. And finally, there was Moonface. His face like the moon as always.

"Safe Shawn," said Moonface, extending a fist to be bumped. Shawn blanked him as he waited for Gullum's clock to reach quarter to six. Moonface dropped his extended arm with a twinge of disappointment. He'd been parred off.

Shawn looked at the group of potheads in front of him. His was disappointed that none of them were girls, but more than happy that they had a market. Not that he showed it. He knew he couldn't trust any of the people in front of him. Especially Moonface.

Quarter to six happened. It was time.

"Well? What are you waiting for?" Shawn scowled at the group in front of him as he pushed the trolley in their direction, "Pay up. In the trolley."

"When do we get the ganje?" the tall bearded dude asked as he tossed his tinned food into the trolley.

"When you've all paid up in full," Shawn replied, keeping an eye on the zombies all around them, "Hurry up, we don't have all day."

The rest put their owed payment into the trolley. Moonface went last. His tins dropped with a loud clang, catching the interest off a nearby zombie. The blonde Nazi-like guy pulled out a taser and fired it straight at the zombie. There was a cracking sound as the zombie twitched on the spot and eventually collapsed. A barbecuey smell arose.

"What the fuck?" Shawn picked up the tins, wondering why they had made such a racket. They were two tins of tomatoes. They were also unusually light. Flipping one over, he found the tin was open. And empty. Shawn didn't even say anything. He just let his pupils fixate upon Moonface.

"Al-al pay you back," Moonface stammered, "I just need it on tick this time. Next time I'll have the food."

Shawn cursed in his mind. Typical Moonface, getting into debt with dealers. Nothing changes, even in a zombie apocalypse. Mentally, he considered his options. He could cause a scene; refuse to give him the bud, set an example. However that was at the risk of attracting unwanted attention. The zombies already looked on edge, more focused than they were before, slowly approaching their position. He had to move or this deal would end in a bloodbath.

"You'd better," he said as he pulled out the green laser pen and flashed it six times into the carousel mirror setup, giving each deal the green light.

"I-I will! I swear!" Moonface continued to blabber, much to the clear disgust of the short Nazi dude who gave him a look of contempt.

"Wait here, my man will be down in two," said Shawn, walking away from the group of uneasy looking potheads.

Meanwhile, at Tommy's house, the green light had gotten through. Dustin, Jeremy and Robin all watched the green light flash six times.

"Shit son, we're a go!" Jeremy said, grinning from ear to ear.

Dustin could hardly believe it. Things were actually working out. If only Casper would glance up from his video game and see their success.

"Well I guess that's me then," said Robin and began making his way down to Street C with a hundred and thirty pounds worth of weed in his drawstring bag.

"You know, this could actually work out," beamed Dustin as Robin turned the corner out of view.

"Yeman, if people keep buying this could be sick," replied Jeremy.

A silence followed as the two of them waited for

Shawn to return with the goods. Robin had switched the radio on whilst they had waited for Shawn's green light which could just about be heard in the background. As usual, Crapital FM was the only damn station still broadcasting.

"Well I'm sure we'll all agree that Zomb Direction's new track is the finest example of next generation music. Call it simple but damn, it was catchy, the crowd outside the studio was loving it! Trying the break into the studio all the way through that track and I think they're still trying now so it's safe to say that these boys will be trending-"

"Safe," said Shawn, pushing the shopping trolley full of tins at Dustin.

"How'd it go?" Jeremy asked as Dustin pushed the trolley into Tommy's house in Casper's general direction.

"As well as it could," Shawn replied as Casper began taking note of their new stock, "I can't believe Moonface is in Gullum."

"I know right, of all the places that fucker could have gone," Jeremy replied.

"I can't believe that waste of skin is alive," Dustin chuckled, "Still, he's helping us out here. I hope he remains a good customer."

"Ah, yeah…" Shawn began, only to be interrupted by Casper.

"Oi! Two of these tins are empty!"

"Wut!?"

"Calm down," said Shawn, not looking very happy, "That 'good customer' wanted his on tick."

"We don't do tick," Dustin frowned.

"Especially not to that wasteman," Jeremy added.

"He's obviously never going to pay us back," Dustin continued, "Did he ever pay Jetlag back? Or That Guy? Or any of the dealers he ticked off?"

"If he doesn't pay us we'll pay him."

"Eh?"

"We'll pay him a visit."

"Oh."

Dustin noticed something out of the corner of his eye. It was red and flashing. It was a red laser light, flashing through their mirror based communication system. Robin was in trouble.

"Fuck."

Whilst Dustin stared at the flashing red laser, his eyes and mind boggling with possibilities, Shawn and Jeremy instantly took off, Jeremy forgetting to grab a weapon. Once they run out of view, Dustin stormed back into Tommy's house.

"What's up?" Casper asked as he was filling in his spreadsheet.

"Red light," Dustin replied whilst rushing into the living room with urgency and grabbing the sword that Jeremy had stolen from Emperor's Portal shopping centre and running back to the kitchen, "Casper! We need to fortify this place, get off your craptop you lazy shit!"

"What's happened?" Casper asked, not moving an inch as Dustin began making sure the house was defendable.

"No idea. Just a red light. Shawn and Jeremy have gone to check it out."

"Yeah, but what's happened?" Casper repeated.

"I dunno! Zombies or maybe some shit stain wanting our supply free of charge! Robin is in trouble! Move!"

Casper did eventually move, helping Dustin ensure the small courtyard outside Tommy's house was both defendable and secure. Ten minutes had passed with no clue as to what was going on down at Street C. Eventually, the three of them returned. But all was not good.

"Get the sofa clear, Robin's been hit!" Shawn yelled as he and Jeremy aided something that had once resembled Robin towards their base. As they entered the house, the extent of the damage was truly revealed. It wasn't nice.

Robin's face had been torn on one side. Half of his jaw was missing and he had no tongue. As he was dragged to the sofa, Dustin couldn't help thinking about the Batman movie that Shawn's brother, Jack, had been watching at the time zombie apocalypse had broken out. It took him a second to work out why he was thinking of Batman as he watched Robin write in pain with half of his face gone, bleeding all over Tommy's sofa. Then he realised. Harvey Twoface.

"Fuck! What do we do!?" yelled Jeremy as Robin bled and cried.

Casper's eyes looked like they were going to pop from his skull.

"Meds!" growled Dustin, "Where does Tommy keep his meds?"

"What the fuck are meds gonna do fam!?" Jeremy shouted back, "He has no fucking face!"

"Least we can do is relieve him from pain!"

"True dat," said Shawn, seemingly calm as ever, "I'll check what they have in the bathroom."

"Casper, go check the kitchen," Dustin instructed, "I'm certain I saw some pills there."

Casper didn't go straight away. He continued to stare at the horribly disfigured Robin with a large degree of alarm for a moment as though he was unable to tear the sight from his vision. Finally he ran out of the room with his eyes closed.

"Who did this?" Dustin pulled a face of disgust as Robin let out a harrowing moan of pain.

"Who do you think?" Jeremy asked as though it was obvious. It wasn't, so he continued, "Zombies fam. When we got there he was surrounded by them, innit. He was on the ground as they…"

"As they?" Dustin pried for more details.

"They were tearing chunks from him," Jeremy replied bitterly, blinking back tears as he gave Dustin a riled stare, "By the time we got them off him… well… they'd pretty much eaten half his face."

"Goddammit."

Tommy didn't have any pills. Nothing they could use anyway. After about ten minutes of debating whether cat worming pills would help Robin, they noticed that Robin wasn't even conscious anymore. He had passed out. Looking at the mess of his face and subsequently the sofa and the rest of Tommy's living room, this could have been because of the pain or the loss of blood. It was safe to say the sofa was ruined now. And the carpet. And parts of the wallpaper. It was time to discuss their next move.

The atmosphere was solemn as they sat around the table in the last of the light of the day.

"Right, obviously we have an issue here," Dustin said, "We need to figure out our options."

"There are no options, he's been bitten," said Casper, refusing to make eye contact with anyone.

"I don't understand," Shawn grumbled, his face in his hands, "The zombies down there were placid as fuck man. They didn't give a shit. And there certainly wasn't that many either. Two or three at most, Robin would have had no trouble batting them off. Especially with all the guys waiting to pick up we had down there."

"Yeah, what happened to them guys?" Jeremy asked, "They were gone."

"They probably had something to do with it," Shawn snarled, standing up suddenly, "This has fucking Moonface written all over it!"

"You're right!" Jeremy stood up too, accidentally sending his chair falling backwards and clattering loudly on the floor.

"He's not!" Dustin protested, wearing a scowl so deep it was practically merging with his eyeballs, "Think about it! Why pay if you're going to steal?"

"Knew this was all a bad idea," Casper muttered to himself to deaf ears.

"Moonface didn't pay!" Jeremy replied, "The fucking cocksucker pulled one on us! Set us up!"

"Yeah!"

"Wait... wait... wait..." Dustin stood up, shaking a dismissive hand, "We can all agree that Moonface is a slimy waste of skin, right?"

Three heads nodded with certainty.

"But we can also agree he's an idiot too right?" Dustin asked.

Three heads all nodded again.

"He's the only guy I know who's been stupid enough to get into thousands of pounds of debt with dealers over weed of all things!" Dustin protested, "This guy doesn't have the intelligence to set up something like this. And as for the rest of them, we don't even know them and they'd already paid! Why kill your dealer after paying them? Doesn't make sense!"

A nasty silence followed.

"None of it makes sense," Shawn agreed quietly as he gently sat down.

A second nasty silence. This one even longer than the last.

"What happens now then?" Jeremy finally asked.

"We admit this drug dealing idea was rubbish," Casper said as though he was having a moment of triumph.

"Shut the fuck up!" Shawn let rip, not even caring if the noise would attract danger, "You're a fucking wasteman! This is serious!"

"Exactly!" Casper argued back, not understanding why Shawn was so angry at him, "And it was all the doing of you guys! Admit you were wrong and stop this stupidity!"

"Casper, I know full well you're only saying that because you oppose the idea," Dustin joined in the debate, "Quit the 'I told you so' attitude because regardless of how the plan went, without us you'd have probably starved to death by now!"

"Just sayin'."

"Well stop just sayin'," Jeremy butted in, "The plan

went fine. We got the food in exchange for bud. We obviously have customers, blud."

"So Robin getting his jaw and half of his face taken from him is just teething problems then?" Casper demanded, doing his 'I am right' arm fold and scowl.

"Exactly. Well, no-"

"Goddammit, this isn't helping. We need to find out if this was zombies or a deliberate act from any survivors," Dustin cut over the argument before it spiralled out of control.

"Zombies," said Jeremy.

"Deliberate," said Shawn at the exact same time.

"How do you suppose we find that out?"

Dustin stared out of one of the few un-boarded windows. It was now dark outside. He could see nothing but the refection of the kitchen. Everybody in the reflection looked tired and hacked off.

"If the zombie count is still low, we could go take a look," said Dustin quietly, "Scout Street C for anything unusual quicktime. Just to be sure."

"Fine," Shawn said, grabbing a weapon, "Me and you can go Dustin. You guys... hold the fort."

"Wait, what if it is zombies?" Casper asked.

"Then we'll have to be extra careful next time," Shawn replied.

"No, no!" Casper appeared very alarmed, "If it's zombies that has done this to him... he's infected, right? Or at least I'm guessing so... I dunno how it works in real life."

Dustin mulled it over in his mind. Casper had a point. How did people become zombies? And if it was the usual way of being bitten to become infected, the standard and less-imaginative approach when it came to zombie fiction, then Robin was probably already dead.

"Fuck."

All eyes turned to the living room door, which remained closed. Jeremy quietly picked up his sword.

"First sign of trouble, you're going to have to do it," said Shawn, his eyes focused on the sword.

"Yeah, don't go thinking a zombie Robin could just be a sleepwalking Robin or clichés like that or we'll all probably end up zombies," Dustin added as they both slipped quietly out of the house, leaving Jeremy and Casper to hope that Robin wasn't infected.

Yet again, the moonlight was doing an effective job at lighting Gullum. It was another clear night and just as well. The street lamps were all dead and they had no torches. Thanks to the moon it seemed brighter outside than it was inside.

Street C looked its usual self. The zombie count was once again low, Shawn only having to dismember the one on the way. Other than two others that appeared to be blindly stumbling in opposite directions, there was little activity. Strewn across the street were several disturbingly still corpses.

"I don't get it," Shawn whispered as the pair peered down Street C, "There was bare of them when we rescued Robin. Like… bare. I took down at least five of them."

"Whoa, bare!" Dustin replied sarcastically.

"Fuck off, there were loads," Shawn said whilst cautiously walking down the street.

"Well, were there loads when you first arrived?"

"Nope. Only a few and most of them were on some next hype."

Dustin pondered a moment as they walked past their advertisement. Even in the dark, he could see they already had new orders for the next day in the few brief hours since the first dealing. The 'I Shower Naked Club' was getting popular.

"So what you're saying is… in the space between you taking payment and Robin arriving with the bud, the place was flooded with zombies?" Dustin asked.

"Exactly that," Shawn replied, "But what caused it? Robin wouldn't have attracted them himself fam.

Something happened here."

No shit, Dustin thought as they continued to search for clues. It didn't take long before Dustin noticed something peculiar. A blinking red light from the corner of his eye, coming from a battered trashcan that stood with disgrace next to a tall and proud lamp post.

Without a word, Dustin jogged straight to the trashcan and peered inside. Within was a load of trash, mainly discarded packaging and body parts. However, placed on top of the small mound of rubbish was Robin's laser pen. Still flashing red. Intrigue flooding his mind, Dustin picked it up.

"Is that-?"

"Robin's laser pen, yeman," Dustin interrupted, still allowing the device to flash, "It was in this bin."

Shawn glanced over to the pool of blood and scattering of body parts around their advertisement poster and carousel mirror at the other end of the street.

"Yeman, I know," Dustin nodded. It was obvious someone had done something. No laser pen walks half a street on its own accord and then jumps into a trash can.

They were just about to move on when Dustin noticed where the laser pen in his hand was flashing. It was flashing directly at the lamp post. Nothing out of the ordinary considering that is where the laser was being aimed at that moment in time, but something caught his attention. It was something attached to the lamp post.

Shawn noticed it too and went to investigate. After a moment of de-attaching whatever it was off the post, he held it up to show Dustin. Squinting in the semi-darkness, Dustin could just about make out what it was. It was a dog collar complete with chain.

"This wasn't here before, I'm certain of it," said Shawn.

"Maybe someone in Gullum still has a dog?" Dustin suggested.

"Had a dog you mean," Shawn replied, taking the collar and chain with him.

"You need that or something?"

"Might be useful, innit."

"True."

It was safe to say that something had certainly gone very wrong on Street C when Robin had arrived. But what exactly went wrong was hard to pinpoint. The 'deliberate' theory was defiantly more plausible.

"Let's get outta here," Shawn said quietly, looking up at the rooftops of Street D, "I dunno why but I feel like were being watched."

Dustin felt like Shawn was chatting shit, but kept his thoughts to himself and joined Shawn back to Tommy's house.

When they returned, they found Jeremy and Casper stood around Robin's mauled body in the living room.

"Should we poke him with a stick?" Casper asked.

"I dunno fam…"

Despite the flippant comments, it was clear to see Jeremy and Casper were both distressed. Many minutes had passed since they had lost the battle to fight back their tears and realisation of Robin's fate dawned between then.

"Still no movement?" Dustin asked.

"I dunno if he's dead or about to turn or just passed out," Jeremy replied as Shawn passed him his sword.

"Pulse?" Shawn asked.

"Do you wanna check?" asked Jeremy, facing Shawn with watery eyes, "I ain't going close."

"FFS," FFS'd Shawn, grasping a fist around Robin's wrist whilst also attempting to retain some distance. No pulse was felt. Robin was dead.

Shawn didn't even have to say anything. The look on his face told the story. Dead as a doornail. Cold as left over pork chops.

"But he didn't change," Jeremy wondered out loud as the four of them stared at Robin's mangled corpse.

"There's still time," said Dustin, his retina's fixed upon the sickening sight in front of him.

For a while, nobody said a word. It was as though they were all expecting a clichéd trap. The possibility that Robin could come back to life as soon as their focus turned had them all transfixed. Then Casper broke the silence.

"M-maybe they don't come back if they're already dead."

"Whaddya mean?" Jeremy demanded.

"W-well if they've already died before the... um... I'm assuming it's an infection- if they die before they're infected, they're dead," Casper explained, "For good I mean."

"So you're saying Robin won't turn?" Shawn asked, his eyes still on Robin's corpse.

"Yes!"

"Makes sense, credible enough," Dustin said almost dismissively, "It's kinda clear that lack of blood got him first here."

'Kinda clear' was an understatement. Anybody new walked in now and they'd assume the living room had been painted red. And the kitchen floor. And the hallway. The place looked like a slaughtering house.

"Weird," said Jeremy quietly, "I expected it to be airborne like-"

"-the endless supply of stupid zombie movies and TV shows?" Dustin interrupted.

"Yeah... like that."

Despite now realising his body was not going to return to life and attack them, the four of them continued to stare at Robin's dead carcass in silence as the night continued its starry advance upon Gullum. Shawn noticed a bulge in Robin's front pocket. Quietly, he reached across and opened it, revealing a fat spliff that Robin had rolled earlier. Remaining silent, he grabbed it and sparked up.

DAY 5

Tensions were high the next day. Not a word had been said of Robin's death. They hadn't even moved him from the sofa. Casper was now sleeping in the attic, a move that made sense since he refused to smoke weed and the plants growing up there were of no interest to him. As they all slowly dragged themselves from their haunted dreams, the Gullum tower clock chimed nine.

As usual, Dustin prepared breakfast. In all the excitement of yesterday, they had forgotten to eat an evening meal. Not that it mattered much. As he scanned the large supply of food they now had, Dustin realised he wasn't very hungry. There was a smell coming from the living room. The smell of unnecessary sacrifice. It stunk.

It appeared everyone else was feeling the same way. They sat in silence around the post-apocalyptic banquet Dustin had prepared for them, not really eating a thing. Dustin felt hollow. Their goods felt ill-gotten.

"It's all our fault," mumbled Jeremy, breaking the awkward silence that was in danger of reaching its fifteenth minute, "If we hadn't pushed that dumb plan, Robin wouldn't be dead."

"You're right," said Casper in his 'I-told-you-so' tone

that Dustin found annoying, "I knew it was a bad idea. I said that all along."

"No," Dustin frowned, more annoyed at Casper being all holier-than-thou than the situation they were in, "It was a good idea. I hate to say this, but Robin's... death... there has to be more to it than we think."

"Dustin's right," Shawn jumped in, "His laser pen was found in a bin at the opposite end of the street. Someone must have fucked shit up for us innit."

"Oh my days guys! Can't you see that if we continue down this road we'll all end up dead!" Casper blurted out, irritated at Dustin's ideas.

"Chances are, if we hadn't made this plan, all of us would be dead by now fam!" sneered Dustin, feeling his impatience rise as Casper's incessant pessimism continue to plague them, "All you ever do is criticize our ideas man! You never come up with your own! Just diss everyone else's!"

"But this plan isn't working! Clearly!" Casper continued to protest.

"Yo!" Shawn was beginning to get impatient with Casper too, "What do you see in front of us, huh? You think all that food just jumped onto the table by itself blud? We have a market here, a market that is willing to pay the price for our product! Stopping now would be stupid! I didn't check it properly but I deffo saw more orders on the poster last night. People want this."

"I'm undecided," an emotionless Jeremy announced as though it would help matters. It didn't.

"It's a no-brainer as far as I'm concerned," said Dustin, attempting to encourage his appetite with some of the tinned 'beef' sausages that had probably never seen a cow in their watery tinned lives, "Today we find out what went wrong and fix it so it doesn't happen again."

There was a pause as the four of them thought their own private ideas filled with regret and what-ifs. Dustin felt slightly sick as his mind turned to Robin's corpse that was still stationary in the Living Room. He could have sworn that the air was thick with the smell of rotting flesh for a horrible moment.

"I'll take over Robin's stuff, shotting 'n' shit," Jeremy mumbled.

"Who's gonna do the promotion and sales then?" Casper demanded, "I'm sure as hell not doing more-"

"Casper, chill," Dustin rubbed his forehead in a defeatist sort of way, "I'll do it. It's only logging sales and making a poster it can be merged with quality assurance."

Wanting to spend as much time away from Casper's pessimism as possible, Shawn and Dustin went down to Street C once again. Jeremy agreed to bag up for the day's sales, leaving Casper to his spreadsheets and conquest for Roman world domination.

Street C looked pretty much the same as it did the night before. Except it was daylight. The zombie count seemed higher than usual, but nothing alarming. They appeared mostly content with minding their own business instead of chasing after fresh meat. As they had walked past the clock tower, Dustin noticed a whole group of about twenty zombies, all furiously pounding their rotting fists against the graffitied walls. He assumed they still took offence to the automated chiming bells that seemed to be powered by thin air.

The trails of blood and body parts were more visible in the daylight. It was now quite easy to envision what had occurred that evening. The only question that remained was how it all occurred. What was the catalyst? What provided the spark that erupted events into action?

Daylight brought a fresher perspective for the pair, but failed to shed any new light upon what had occurred. The mystery behind the moving laser pen and collar and chain remained unresolved.

"Fuck," Shawn spat, wearing a frown big enough to put a dampener on the whole day.

Dustin knew why Shawn was so angry. They were

clueless as they stood in the centre of Street C, next to the bin and lamppost that had sparked their interest previously. As he looked around, Dustin knew something was wrong. Something had changed. Something subtle. Something otherwise overlooked. And not knowing was driving him insane.

Sunlight in his eyes, Dustin turned slowly to the house wall that the lamppost was proudly stood in front of. There was some graffiti.

FUCK PESK RUDE

Could it be? Dustin's mind was racing as he walked over to the graffitied house wall. He had no idea what the three words meant, but at least one of the words and the near unreadable scrawl it had been sprayed in seemed somewhat familiar. Unsure what was coming over him as Shawn watched with disbelieving eyes, Dustin bent down and sniffed the graffiti.

Pupils widened as realisation hit. Dustin stood up sharply.

"This paint is still fresh," he said without turning.

"Y'wot?"

"This paint," Dustin grinned, spinning on the spot to face Shawn, "It's recent! This... Pesk... guy, he's a survivor! This graffiti wasn't here yesterday!"

"So what are you saying? It was him? This 'Pesk' person?" Shawn asked.

"Maybe. Either way, I think it's worth checking out. He may know something."

"Wait," Shawn's frown hadn't moved, "How do you suppose we find this guy? Follow the-"

"-graffiti?"

"I'm sure I've seen this guy's name written in Sinthwaite and Morrhead Centre. Probably even in Puddock too. He could be anywhere! He is everywhere!" complained Shawn, "You could walk from here to Lower

Gullum and see that word at least a dozen times."

"True…" Dustin kept his thoughts to himself for a moment, looking around the decimated remains of Gullum as Shawn beat off a rouge zombie that had spotted them, "I'm not the tinfoil hat sort… but I'm going to have to say this was deliberate. Someone wanted this to happen. Someone is toying with us. And by the looks of it, it's probably a graffiti… um… 'artist.'"

"Yo! Some help!" Shawn called as he struggled to fight away the rouge zombie. Dustin swung his golf club, narrowly avoiding Shawn's snooker cue and hitting the zombie square on the cheekbone. Despite a satisfying bone-crunching sound, Dustin's attack had little effect.

"Weak arse bastard," Shawn cursed, wrestling the undead off him and dropping his snooker cue with a large clatter. The echo echoed louder than the pair of them wanted and before either of them could react, zombie activity had increased either side of the street. They were trapped.

"Shit! Down here!" Dustin pointed towards a narrow snicket between two houses as the zombies picked up their pace to a run. Dustin sprinted towards their escape route, but Shawn stopped to grab his snooker cue.

"Fuck the cue! Fuck the cue!" Dustin yelled whilst pulling Shawn away, nearly dropping his golf club in the process. With the zombies now approaching at an alarming pace, Shawn decided it would indeed be best to 'fuck the cue' and bolted down the gap in the houses with Dustin.

Their escape plan wasn't the best. As soon as they had entered the ally, zombies from Street D began flooding down towards them. They were trapped by a sudden horde. And Shawn no longer had his weapon.

"Goddammit!"

"Fuck's sake! This is so clichéd!" moaned Shawn as the pair desperately looked for a way out.

As danger drew closer, Dustin scanned one the

buildings they were stuck between. Like most of the buildings in Gullum, 'Pesk' had been hard at work on one of them. In fact, the word had been written so many times in this particular wall that whoever 'Pesk' was may as well have just painted it all black.

Dustin looked up. As if luck would have it, this particular building had a broken fire escape. There was a broken set of rusty metal stairs leading to the roof. Unfortunately, they were about twenty feet from the ground. With the zombies hurtling towards them at full speed now, screaming horribly with every pace, he knew they had to do this quicktime.

Without even asking, Dustin leaped onto Shawn's back and then jumped up to the stairs, ignoring Shawn's protests and efforts to ditch him. For a truly horrible second, Dustin was convinced he wasn't going to make it, doomed by physics to crash land back to the hard ground. Fortunately, with the golf club, he managed to hook the club head with the bottom step.

Seconds remained before the two riotous armies of zombies crashed into one another and Shawn. Dustin stretched a hand out. Shawn jumped. Their hands clasped. The two zombie gangs clashed and began tearing chunks from each other. They were safe. As long as Dustin could hang on to both Shawn and the golf club.

"I'm not built for this," Dustin growled through clenched teeth over the haunting noise below, sweat pouring from his forehead as his foetus-like muscles began to shake with the strain.

Shawn looked down at the riot below. Dead body parts and stale blood was on sale it seemed.

"You better not fucking let go!" Shawn hissed as he began to climb up Dustin, who was going bright red in the face.

"Hurry!" groaned Dustin as Shawn climbed over his head and onto the rickety steps before dragging Dustin up.

A moment of elation swept over them as the pair

gasped for breath on the staircase. Anybody passing would have thought they had been satisfying some sort of strange post zombie apocalypse fetish.

Dustin closed his eyes, focusing his mind on the gentle heat from the sun and the sounds of carnage below. That had been a close one. Too close. A few seconds longer of hanging there and he just may have let go. Skinny dipping in a sea of zombies. Fully clothed.

His strange daydream was cut short by a strange feeling of coldness by his neck. He opened his eyes to find an unfamiliar blonde haired and blue-eyed man holding a stupidly big knife to his neck. Glancing to his side, Dustin saw Shawn was in the same predicament, a slightly stockier brown haired male was holding him down. Both appeared to be dressed in leather jackets, which gave the impression that they took themselves a little too seriously.

"Goddammit!" Dustin sighed.

"Now wot we got here then, sweetie?" Mr blonde-hair grinned.

"Something ugly by the looks of it," Shawn replied, fucks not given to their situation.

The knife wielding pair glanced at each other, a look of almost disbelief in their eyes.

"Sorry cupcake, didn't quite catch that!" Mr brown-hair said loudly with forced enthusiasm, pressing the large knife harder against Shawn's neck.

Before anybody could do or say anything, there was an intense shudder. A zombie had managed to leap into reach of the stairs and was now hanging off the bottom step. The entire staircase began to creak as though it was about to give way and collapse as the zombie snarled in the ears of Dustin and Shawn.

"Jesus H Christ son!" Mr brown-hair seemed to mockingly mimic an American accent, "We gotta ged our asses outta here boi!"

"Spray 'em," Mr blonde-hair replied.

Mr brown-hair pulled out what looked like a small

aerosol can and sprayed it right into Shawn's face, who passed out nearly immediately. The can was passed over and before he could even react, Dustin received his dose. The world slipped away into a muddy haze.

*

It was the smell that first hit their pair of them as they drifted back into consciousness. And it was defiantly the smell of rotting flesh. The stench violated their nostrils like a slap to the face. It helped bring them round from the land of asleep, but it was far from pleasant.

The second thing Dustin noticed was the cell bars. And how they were probably on the wrong side of them. Scanning the room, he noticed several other cells circling a bare oblong room. The only source of light was coming from a skylight on the roof, which shone the bright summer rays onto a desk that appeared to be spilling over with junk. Spray cans, marker pens, candles, a paperback copy of The Munchies Games, several old Blackberry's, piles of white powder and a few overflowing ashtrays occupied the small amount of desk space provided. Someone had graffitied the entire room, mostly with the word 'Pesk' amongst a few others. It took him a few minutes to realise where they were. It was the Gullum Police Station. But most importantly, Dustin noticed a dog collar and chain, partially hidden by some of the desks junk. Seemed they were about to meet their tormentors.

He glanced over at Shawn who appeared to be sat up and a little more conscious than himself.

"Shhhh," shhh'd Shawn gently as Dustin was about to say something. Shaking slightly, he pointed to the centre of the room. Dustin focused. There were people here.

Four people to be exact. All men. The two thugs who had brought them here were stood either side of the desk. A third man was sat behind the desk. He was very skinny, wore a grey beanie hat and had a crackhead sort of vibe about him as he continuously scratched and itched his body. The fourth person looked like he'd just finished work on a building site. He appeared to be dressed in a scruffy high visibility outfit that was covered in dust and was facing the other three, his back to the door. It seemed that some sort of debate or argument was occurring.

"So you're this 'Pesk' guy then?" the building site man frowned. There was a negative mood in the air, but nobody there appeared intimidated.

'Pesk' said nothing and continued to scratch himself from behind the desk.

"Fancy speaking darling?" the man continued to speak, adjusting his tone as though his audience were stupid.

"Look sweetie, Pesk says what he wants when he wants-" Mr blonde-hair began.

"Go fuck yourself 'National Front'. Who the fuck do you think you are?" the man stood up and casually strolled over to the blonde with open arms, demonstrating how much better built he was, "You two are as unlovable as them twats who present Homes Under The Hammer. Fucking. Keep. Out. Of. This!"

"Fuck! Pesk! Rude!" Pesk spat, twitching and itching as though he had a form of Tourette's syndrome, "Bullshit! This was Kristoff and Reece's idea! They told me what you've been doing. You have something we want."

"Heh. Better do better than that darling! The 'I know what you did last summer' routine ain't washing lad."

"Kristoff!" Pesk said sharply in what seemed to be his usual staccato tone, "Explain."

Mr blonde-hair, or Kristoff, began explaining.

"Look sweetie, we know you're Duke. Big time MD dealer before all this kicked off. Ring any bells fam? Anyway, we've been watching you take your supply with you as you raid every pub in Sinthwaite, Cuxley, Lower Gullum and now Upper Gullum in your shitty red Ford Focus. Been living it up have we? Post apocalypse pub-crawl? We've been watching you do your thing all around the valley."

Pesk grinned and gestured towards Kristoff as though his words had explained everything, "C'mon then blud!"

"Wot?" Duke neither looked intimidated or clued up as to what was occurring.

Pesk's hands slammed down upon the desk, sending an ashtray falling to the floor and making Dustin and Shawn jump slightly, "The MD! Where is it?"

"I dunno darlin'. I guess it could be in any of the pubs I've visited," Duke sneered, rubbing a hand through the gingery fluff on his head that he once may have called hair, "You ought to know, you were watching me."

"Fuck!" Pesk twitched violently, "Fuck! Fuck! Fuck! Fuck! Fuck! Fuck! Fuck! FUCK! Fuck!"

Dustin's eyes widened as he watched Pesk's twitching and swearing fit in front of them all. But it didn't stop there. Continuing his furious chant of the word 'fuck,' he picked up a spray can off the desk and began spray-painting his name on the wall repetitively. By the end of his outburst, Pesk was pretty much screaming the word 'fuck,' whilst painting over and over his own name. It was a crazy sight. Dustin had met some crazy people in his time but Pesk was something else. He seemed truly unhinged.

"Finished?" Duke smiled, looking amused at Pesk's little breakdown as the madman dropped his spray can and returned to sit behind the desk, "Looks like you've snorted a bit too much for your own good darlin'."

Pesk stared at the desk for a moment before focusing back on Duke, "Oh, I'm only just getting started. Bring him here!"

"Right, let's get this over with" said Mr brown-hair who was assumingly known as Reece as the pair of them revealed their large knives and calmly walked over to Duke.

Duke didn't say a word as Kristoff and Reece dragged

him over to Pesk's desk at knifepoint. Pesk stood up and grabbed Duke by the chin.

"It was a mistake for you to come to Gullum," he spat in Duke's face.

"Was it?" Duke still appeared unfazed by the events.

"You're in trouble," Pesk continued, "Big trouble."

Duke almost laughed before he spoke, "Dunno if you've noticed darlin', but the entire sodding world's in big trouble."

Pesk continued to glare.

"Now. You can stop pretending you're going to kill me," Duke continued, shrugging the knifes off and calmly standing up, "If you want MD that bad darlin', I'm willing to sell."

Pesk continued to glare. Dustin watched his glare turn into a manic grin. It took him a moment to realise what had occurred as the pair of them watched from behind bars. Finally Duke's face gave it away. The confident smirk had turned to an expression of pain and confusion. He looked down at his broad chest to find several inches of Kristoff's knife poking out of it. He had been stabbed in the back.

"Who said anything about buying?" Pesk snarled grabbing the sides of Duke's face as blood began to pour from his mouth. Duke didn't make another sound. Kristoff ripped the knife from his body and Pesk let him fall to the floor.

"Right then," Reece sighed, folding his arms and staring down at the dead Duke, "Another one bites the dust."

"Want us to check out the car?" Kristoff asked Pesk who had sat back down. He waved a hand dismissively, not even looking up at Kristoff. Reece and Kristoff must have taken it as a yes since they both promptly strolled out of the room, dragging Duke's body by the legs.

Now the pair of them found themselves alone with Pesk and a pint of Duke's blood. Pesk appeared to ignore them at first, which came across as a relief to Dustin at least. The possibly psychotic weirdo remained in his seat, staring at the skylight for a little while, scratching all the time.

"Yo," Shawn broke the ice, "Dafuq man?"

Dustin mentally cursed. Duke had hardly been a pushover, in fact, whilst watching, Dustin had his money on Duke throughout. What had made Shawn think he could 'badman' his way out of this? They were clearly way out of their depth.

Pesk jumped up from his seat, near enough immediately and before the two of them could even blink he was in front of them, peering at them from behind the bars. The staring lasted a while.

"What?" Shawn demanded as Pesk continued to stare.

"He's like a skinny little old baby cow, isn't he?" Pesk grinned, eyeing up Dustin with an expression that seemed close to fascination, "You ever slice an ear of a baby cow? They scream and scream. It's funny."

"Was that some sort of threat-y thing?" Dustin asked, confused as to how baby cows were any way relevant to the situation, "How is it even possible to have an old baby?"

"Smart guy, huh?"

"Yes. And you're the bad guy, I get it," Dustin replied, "You're the one who killed Robin. Or at least had Robin killed."

Pesk stared blankly at Dustin as though he had no idea what he was on about. Finally after pulling a series of confused facial expressions, he spoke, "Who's Robin?"

"That guy you had chewed up by zombies yesterday," Shawn scowled, "You left your zombie controlling collar and leash behind. And your name."

"Ohhhhhh!" Pesk jumped up and clapped his hands as though something had just clicked in his head, "You're the 'I Shower Naked Club!'"

Dustin and Shawn stared in disbelief as Pesk grinned

at them as though he had just met his favourite idol.

"You guys are brilliant, sheer genius!" Pesk continued to rave with admiration, "Selling draws to survive, I'd have never though of such a great idea, here, shake my hand, I beg of ya!"

Dustin found himself looking at Pesk's outstretched and veiny hand reach through the cell bars. Cautiously, he reached out to shake his hand.

"POW!" Pesk yelled as he punched Dustin across his face before his hand could be shook.

Dustin was flung to the back of the cell by the sheer force of Pesk's punch. Hurting, Dustin glared back at Pesk, rubbing his jaw. Meanwhile, Shawn remained silent.

"You gotta be joking blud!" Pesk roared with amusement, surprisingly articulate as the words rolled off his tongue quicker otters on a bank, "What'd you think you are some sort of badman because you shot draws now blud? You think we're just gonna stand for that, huh? I knows things blud, I knows things! And I knows you yewts weren't nowhere to be seen before the zombies began. Think you can just take man's custom cos the dead don't die anymore!?"

Pesk's furious eyes burned holes into the pair of them. Metaphorically of course.

"Actually… yeah," Shawn replied calmly, ensuring he was well out of hitting reach.

"Well not anymore! This ends now famalams or I end you both now! I'm gonna fuck, fuck, fuck, fuck-" Pesk returned to his repetitive manic state, "-fuck, fuck, fuck, fuck, fuck, fuck, fuck-"

The pair of them watched with disbelief once again as the nutter returned to his desk with great strides, grabbed a spray paint can and began screaming expletives and spraying his name on the walls once again.

"-fuck, fuck, fuck, fuck, fuck, fuck-pesk-rude-fuck-pesk-rude-fuck-pesk-rude-FUCK-PESK-RUDE-FUCK-PESK-RUDE-FUCK-PESK-RUDE!" he screamed before his little episode ended, "NOW HOW THE FUCK DOES THAT SOUND!?"

"Quite mad," replied Dustin thoughtfully as he clicked his throbbing jaw back into position.

Pesk was about to make a screw-face, usually a bad sign for violent people like him. However, Kristoff and Reece returned with news. Bad news.

"We've been tricked sweetie," Kristoff said, slightly sullen as he revealed a tiny bag of white powder and a scrap of paper.

"What does it say!?" Pesk demanded as he threw his spray paint can back upon the cluttered desk.

"'I could have saved you more darling, but let's face it, you're a fucking wasteman,'" Reece read the note Duke must have left in a monotonous voice, "'Have this line on me. Kiss.'"

Pesk snatched the button bag that contained a small line of Duke's MD in it off Kristoff and closely inspected it.

"Looks like he knew we were watching him," said Kristoff, "He must have shifted it all before we got to him."

"Or sniffed it," replied Reece.

"Yeman," agreed Kristoff, "That's one sweet way to go out. Get smashed and then hand yourself in when you've run out of gear and pubs to go to."

"Fridge and Magnet!" Pesk glared at Kristoff.

"Fine," Kristoff replied, "Coming with or are you wanting time with our little Heisenbergs there?"

"They're coming too," Pesk sniffed, "Gullum will be f-f-fuckking mine by the end of today."

The pair of them had their hands taped together and were pulled from the cells, before being dragged to Duke's car outside. Whatever was occurring, Dustin hadn't been expecting this. He glanced over to Shawn as a zombie pointlessly attempted to break into the car. It didn't look like Shawn knew much about what was going on either.

Kristoff sat at the wheel with Dustin next to him in the passenger seat. Between Reece and Pesk in the back was Shawn. Pesk was looking as on edge as ever as his pupils darted about all over the place. Without a word, Kristoff started Duke's spluttering and rusting hulk of a car and began driving. Several zombies became croppers on the way, leaving some nasty red stains upon the windscreen. It seemed as the days passed, the zombies were getting less agile and more decomposed.

They were driven to the top end of Upper Gullum, a few blocks past Tommy's house were Jeremy and Casper were still assumingly waiting for their return. On the way they narrowly missed being hit by a grey Renault Clio that was driving down to Lower Gullum at breakneck speeds. It seems they weren't the only ones driving about. Or being driven about at least.

"Who the fucks that?" Pesk asked. Nobody knew.

At the top of Upper Gullum, just before the barren wasteland that was the endless Morrhead moors, was The Fridge and Magnet, Gullum's only pub. As they pulled up alongside it, Dustin couldn't help thinking that last orders had already been called.

"Out," Pesk pretty much shoved poor Shawn out of the car, who fell upon the tarmac. He quickly scrabbled to get up, a task made much harder by the tape locking his hands together.

Without another word, Kristoff grabbed Shawn as Reece pulled Dustin out of the car. Pesk walked up to the heavy wooden doors of the pub as Kristoff and Reece decapitated a few of the zombies who had taken an interest in their activities. Unable to defend his face and keep balance at the same time, Dustin found himself with black zombie blood in his eye.

Not caring enough to knock, Pesk pushed the doors open.

The Fridge and Magnet was a cosy affair and would have looked really warm and welcoming if it was possible to switch the lights on and maybe get the fireplace lit. Thanks to this and the flooding of white natural light pouring from the windows, the wood and stone bar area felt abandoned and cold. Guest ales and fizzy lagers were dimly displayed on the bar pumps, most no doubt connected to empty barrels as the serious drinkers kept up their habit in the recent panic.

As they skirted the room, voices called out from around the corner of the bar. Dust danced in the air as they cautiously approached. There were three people there, all male and drinking in front of piles of white powder. One of them looked to be passed out on his bar stool, a small amount of puke dribbling from his mouth and entering the labyrinth that was his mangy beard. The other two were having a conversation and didn't appear to notice the new patrons.

"Look lad, I'll tell you what I said to the lad," one of them mouthed off to the other, "I said lad, you gonna be ladding around like that lad over there and my lad might just have summat to say to ya lad."

"Nice one lad, what'd the lad have to say?" number two replied.

"Ya not gonna believe it lad, you know what the lad said?" the story continued as the four of them approached the three intoxicated survivors, "He said, lad, I'm not ladding you about here lad but some lad is gonna have to tell that lad that no lad is gonna take his ladding around. He'll end up like that lad from Puddock, y'know what I'm saying lad, lad?"

"Lad," number two agreed.

"Hands on balls, bums on walls," Pesk interrupted as Reece instantly pulled the passed out guy's head up from the bar and ran his blade across his throat. Blood sprayed across the bar, most of it contaminating one of the piles of MD.

The two surviving drinkers turned in surprised, unsure whether to be more surprised at the brutal execution of their fellow bar buddy or the presence of Pesk.

"What'd you do that for?" Kristoff asked Reece, looking surprised himself.

"Hated that cunt," Reece replied, keeping a firm grip on Dustin, "Always wanted to kill him. That's the last time he takes my lighter."

"Fair play sweetie."

"Where's Duke, lad?" drinker number one demanded, looking somewhat panicked.

"Fuck you," Pesk replied, pushing him off his bar stool and revealing the mountain of MD in front of him.

"H-hey, that's mine lad!" number one called from the floor as number two saw his chance to escape, running straight outside into the zombie infested world in a mad alarmed rush. He didn't even bother closing the door, leaving the task to Kristoff.

Pesk pulled out a large key and scooped some of the MD up. He put the key to his nose and sniffed deeply, wincing as he did so. He spent a mere second with his eyes closed, waiting for the effects of the drugs to kick in.

"Boomyar!" he yelled, twitching slightly, "Fuck, fuck, fuck, fuck, FUCK, YES! Duke's stuff is always the best!"

"Look lad, the MD is mine-"

Before anybody could react, Pesk had pulled the only remaining drinker from the floor and pinned him to the bar, grabbing his face just like he had done with Duke, "I disagree. You looking at me funny fam?"

"N-no..." the drinker's eyes filled with fear as Pesk's pupils grew ever wider.

"You sure because I could have sworn you looked at me funny," Pesk growled, looking furious at the poor drinker, "I think you'd better give me all of your drugs to make up for it blud."

"N-no..."

"I really hope you didn't just say no to me blud," Pesk glared, his crooked teeth showing, "I don't like it when people say no to me."

"N-no…"

Pesk flipped. Before he knew it, the drinker had been flattened on the floor and Pesk was laying punches to his face.

"Fuck. Pesk. Rude," he chanted with every bone-crunching punch he threw, "Fuck! Pesk! Rude! Fuck! Pesk! Rude! Fuck Pesk Rude! Fuck Pesk Rude! Fuck-Pesk-Rude-Fuck-Pesk-Rude-Fuck-Pesk-Rude-Fuckpeskrudefuckpeskrudefuckpeskrudefuckpeskrudefuck peskrudeFUCKPESKRUDEFUCKPESKRUDE!"

With every punch the poor drinker's face more and more began to resemble a squashed tomato, blood appearing and then sent flying by Pesk's fists as he chanted the three short and meaningless words obsessively. A harrowing sight for both Shawn and Dustin.

"NOW HOW THE FUCK DOES THAT SOUND!?" Pesk roared immediately after his chant, sticking his blood soaked fist in the direction of the four onlookers.

This time, Dustin said nothing, unable to drag his popping eyeballs from the crumpled remains of the drinker's head. They had been in there a total of two minutes and there were already two extremely brutal deaths. And no doubt the stranger that got away was currently being torn to pieces by the zombies outside.

"Fuckin' hell," Kristoff pulled out a set of sandwich bags as he walked towards the mountains of MD sat upon the bar, "Feel better after that?"

Pesk didn't answer the question. He simply walked out of the pub and into the car whilst muttering something about notches on his belt. Kristoff collected the MD and Reece escorted Dustin and Shawn to Pesk. Dustin tried to free an arm from the iron-lock grip Reece had. His attempt didn't get far, he couldn't escape. He glanced over to Shawn to see his eyes telling a similar story. These guys were strong and the 'I Shower Naked Club' was in deep trouble.

"Now then," Pesk glared at them from the driver seat

mirror as Reece sat between them in the back, "You're going to tell me where your yard is."

Kristoff jumped into the passenger seat with the MD in three bulging sandwich bags. A zombie randomly collapsed upon the boot of the car and slid to the ground.

After a moment's silence and heavy glaring off Pesk, Dustin told him the location of Carpathian Mills.

"Do you take man for some kinda flappy bird?" Pesk roared, almost crushing Dustin's jaw as he grabbed the bottom of his face, "You're operating in Gullum so give me a Gullum address!"

A second heavy silence loomed. One that spoke of a possible painful death if Pesk didn't get the answer he wanted. Shawn wisely told him Tommy's house address.

"Winner, winner, chicken dinner," Pesk grinned as he started the bent old car and sent it skidding down towards Tommy's house.

*

The day had been long and slow for Jeremy and Casper. Jeremy had spent the day preparing for the sales. It had been a dull day of watching the zombies walk by and tear limbs from each other as he weighed out weed and stuffed it into button bags. Meanwhile, Casper had been busy slaughtering onslaughts of computerised barbarian invasions amongst lengthy periods of moaning about their situation and citing doom and gloom for them all unless they listened to him. Jeremy did listen, but he wasn't replying. He was contemplating throwing the ginger fuck and his craptop out into the wild world when he heard the distinct sound of a car pulling up close.

"There's a car Jeremy," Casper's distinct voice floated up the stairs as Jeremy watched the red Ford Focus pull up right outside Tommy's house. He ignored Casper and continued watching the car. Five men got out and he immediately identified two of them as Dustin and Shawn.

"This is serious," Jeremy muttered, dropping the weed he was holding and rushing downstairs, nearly falling down it as he did so and saving his neck with the banister which immediately came loose from the wall.

Ignoring the damage and the clouds of plaster pluming from the walls, Jeremy rushed past Casper and his moaning in the kitchen and straight to the front door. The sunlight hit him like a blinding wall of solid whiteness. It was a scorching summer, much warmer than anything before. A moment of blindness and an outstretched hand attempting to block the powerful rays shine down upon him finally subsided as his eyes adjusted to the light.

Before Jeremy could react to the sight of Pesk and his two minions holding Dustin and Shawn hostage, Pesk strode right up to Jeremy and grabbed him by the throat.

"I want to shower naked," he grinned at Jeremy with pupils the size of snooker balls, "Can I join your club?"

Jeremy squirmed under pressure of Pesk's iron clamp grip, struggling to breathe, he managed to squeeze out a word, "S-sure…"

"Yeman that's the right answer," Pesk replied, dropping Jeremy as he strode into Tommy's house, "Come."

They were escorted into kitchen where Casper was still sat at his craptop, watching some sort of video that sounded somewhat inappropriate.

"What the fuck?" Jeremy asked Shawn quietly as Kristoff and Reece pushed the three of them into kitchen.

"Yeah blud what the fuck?" Pesk interrupted before Shawn could answer, "Think you can just rob man's territory…"

Pesk stopped speaking, becoming aware of Casper sat next to him, still watching a video.

"Who are you?" he blurted out at Casper, looking insulted at the lack of attention Casper appeared to be giving the whole situation. It seemed like a hostile takeover of their operations wasn't worth Casper's time.

"Casper," Casper replied, still watching the video. Pesk looked in on what he was watching. It was a porn movie. A moment was spent watching two people who had probably only just met copulate each other. It was a convincing act.

"Oooohh! Yeah! Fuck!" Pesk cried with delight with so much enthusiasm his behaviour resembled sarcasm, "That's someone's daughter that! That's someone's fucking daughter! Look at her take it! She's having a super slag session!"

"She's only just getting started," Casper replied, his eyes still glued upon the hardcore action, "I've got another fifty gigabytes of her. Urthgurl never leaves cyberspace."

"Fuck, fuck, fuck, fuck, Pesk, fuck!" Pesk spat with enthusiasm at the video as though he wanted to jump into the screen and join in on he action himself, "Look at the ayuss! Shame about his limp shit. Should'a been me there, mines like a baby's arm."

"Let's see sweetie," Kristoff wanted in too, pushing through Dustin and Shawn to take a glimpse himself.

It was Kristoff's movements that snapped Pesk out of his sudden porn obsession and back onto his hostile takeover of their operations. Suddenly realising that he was getting distracted, Pesk slammed the craptop's lid shut.

"Nuff," he growled, staring them all out with a look of animosity, "Reece, Kristoff, keep an eye on these goons. I'm gonna check this place out."

And with that, Pesk climbed the stairs, leaving the four of them with Kristoff and Reece, who were holding their large knives with threatening intent. Silence followed as movement was heard from upstairs. Then a small crashing sound that was probably the breaking of a vase. Then a cheering as the mental-case assumingly found their supply of weed.

"These guys have the piff!" Pesk's delighted voice floated down the stairs.

"Guessing you found Robin's murderer then," Jeremy muttered quietly.

"Got summat to say sweetie?" Kristoff asked, placing his blade under Jeremy's neck.

"Not to you," Jeremy replied.

"Dafuq you just say?" Reece demanded, pointing his knife directly at Jeremy's cheek.

"I have something to say," Dustin interrupted, attracting the attention of the knives, "Just a question actually. I mean, I can see you guys are quite intelligent. Why are you following that loon?"

Kristoff and Reece looked at each other.

"What you tranna say sweetie?"

"Well, let's face it, you guys could easily take him out," Dustin continued, hoping to some fictional all-seeing power that his suggestion wouldn't be met with a premature death, "And I think we have room for two more people here. Join us. We have plenty of weed, plenty of food and could really do with your expertise. It could work."

There was another silence followed as Kristoff and Reece stared at each other once more. Everybody else's eyes were on Dustin.

Finally, Reece spoke, "What makes you think he's in charge?"

"W-what? There's somebody above him?" Shawn asked.

"No, not like that sweetie," Kristoff replied with a sly smirk, "He thinks he's taking over Gullum today. But really it's us that's taking over Gullum. We're just letting him do all the work for us first."

"Ah…"

The conversation was interrupted by Pesk leaping down the stairs with two Didl bags of weed, almost tripping over the broken banister rail as he bounded into the kitchen with excitement.

"Nice little setup you boys have here," he beamed,

"Man's gonna get soooo high tonight!"

"What happens now then?" Reece asked, looking bored at everything.

"Oh, kill them," Pesk waved a dismissive arm, "We're done here."

"Righty-oh then sweeties," Kristoff attempting to encourage them to their own slaughter as Pesk began twitching again.

"Let's get this over with."

"Wait, you don't mean me do you?" Casper began to panic, "I'm nothing to do with all this-"

"Oh yeah?" Pesk bent down and glared at Casper with his humongous pupils, "Why you here then fam?"

"We're here because this is our house," Dustin replied as Kristoff and Reece began dragging Jeremy and Shawn towards the front door. They were both attempting to fight back, but Pesk's companions proved too strong.

"Did you just answer me back blud?" Pesk snapped, grabbing both Dustin's and Casper's arms and peering down at Dustin, "Cos man could have sworn you just answered me back!"

"No..." fear was beginning to rise in Dustin's stomach as Casper became even more pale than usual.

"Did you just say no to me blud?" Pesk's eyes were almost on stalks as he released his grip on Casper and prepared his fist for another bloody adventure, "I don't like it when people say no to me..."

Dustin looked at Casper pleadingly, attempting to indicate that he should hit Pesk with his craptop. Or a chair. Or Jeremy's sword if it was still about. Just something.

Unfortunately for him, Casper did sweet fuck all as the killer word slipped from Dustin's lips, "No..."

They were fucked. Jeremy and Shawn were now likely being strung up outside by Kristoff and Reece, probably being fed to the zombies piece by piece. And with Casper's inability to do anything, Dustin was now about to face a five-finger death punch. Fucked they were.

"WAIT!" Dustin screamed at Pesk's fist as it was inches from impact. Pesk paused. Dustin breathed deep.

"WHAT!?" Pesk growled deeply, his maddening stare looking somewhat unhinged.

"You do realise that your bum boys are plotting against you right?"

"What?" Pesk repeated, his expression changing from rage to confusion.

"Kristoff and Reece are just using your influence and infrastructure," Dustin elaborated, "After they've got everything they want, they're gonna turn on you."

"How dare you question the loyalty of MY BOYS!" Pesk began with a low growl and ended by pretty much screaming in Dustin's face, spittle flying from his teeth and lips as he roared.

By this point, Dustin was preparing for fist impact. However, that never happened. Instead, a nasty crunching sound occurred. Pesk's expression dropped blank. He let out what seemed like a strained moan before blood spilled from his mouth and he collapsed on top of Dustin.

"Aw fuck!" Dustin cried as he wiped mouth-blood from his face and pushed the unconscious Pesk off him. Looking up, he was surprised to see Casper looking shaken up and pale, holding the blade of Jeremy's sword. The handle had blood on it.

"Finally, thanks," said Dustin, looking at Casper then the immobile Pesk on the floor, "Why didn't you use the blade?"

"I didn't want to hurt him!" Casper exclaimed as though doing such a thing would have been unforgivable.

Before either of them could do anymore, the front door burst open and Jeremy and Shawn sprinted upstairs. Seconds later, Kristoff and Reece chased after, not even noticing that Pesk had been knocked out, both tripping over the broken banister as they rushed the steps.

"Shit," Dustin turned to Casper, "We'd better help."

Casper said nothing, keeping a firm grip upon the sword blade whilst somehow not cutting his fingers.

"Dafuq?"

Casper shook his head, "I'm not going anywhere with you guys! If it wasn't for you I'd be still at home playing Total War without drug gangs trying to kill us all!"

"If you're not going to help give me the sword then!" Dustin demanded, his patience slipping as he wiped more blood from his face.

Casper shook his head once more. He waved the sword about aimlessly in an attempt to ward Dustin away, almost taking a chunk out of the staircase and Dustin's face as he did so.

"Goddammit! Fucks sake!"

Dustin sprinted up the stairs, leaving Casper on his own with a sword and an unconscious Pesk. Jeremy, Shawn, Kristoff and Reece were in Tommy's room. Attempting to keep quiet, Dustin peeked through the crack of the ever-so-slightly-open-door. From what he could tell, Shawn was bleeding heavily from his nose and Jeremy had the beginnings of a black eye starting to show. Kristoff and Reece had them both surrounded, holding their trademark blades.

"This ends here sweetie," said Kristoff, pacing the room in a threatening manner, "Gullum is ours after today."

Dustin knew what he had to do. He had an emergency weapon stored within Tommy's room. All he had to do was wait. Wait for the right moment. He kept his eye on Kristoff's movements.

"Why won't you just agree to join us?" Jeremy asked, rubbing his sore eye.

"Fuck that, these cunts are not joining the group," Shawn replied, giving one of Pesk's 'boys' a dirty look.

"Why share that you can simply take?" Reece chuckled.

"Exactly sweetie," Kristoff walked to the left where

Reece was at, "Once we have you out of the way, we'll deal with Pesk and then it's all ours!"

"Fuck you," Shawn replied.

"Yeah, eat shit and die!" Jeremy added.

"Wait, did you guys leave the front door open?" Shawn suddenly thought, realising the risk of being flooded with zombies with all the noise they were making was a plausible one.

After a split second's thought, Kristoff walked over towards the window. Dustin grabbed his chance. As soon as he saw Kristoff directly under the light shade that hid the unusable bulb that would have once lit the room at night, he reached his arm into the room and pulled the string that activated his emergency weapon.

The light shade tipped as Kristoff was directly underneath it, revealing the giant Buddha Dustin had taken as a weapon on day one. The precariously balanced object dropped down from the light shade and landed right onto Kristoff's head, with unexpected results.

Instead of just knocking him out, Buddha made mincemeat of Kristoff's head, sending chunks of head and brains flying in all directions as the statue replaced his head with a vile squelch. There was a moment of shock amongst them all as Kristoff's body stumbled as his neck continued to bleed, the Buddha still balanced on what remained of his head. He collapsed on the floor, sending the blood stained statue rolling under Tommy's bed somewhere.

Reece, his mouth wide open and face covered in bits of Kristoff turned to the door where Dustin was. Knowing he had been spotted, Dustin fled to Tommy's parent's room.

"Motherfucker," Reece snarled as he chased after him.

Inside Tommy's parent's bedroom, Dustin searched frantically for Jeremy's emergency weapon. His quick sweep of the room found nothing as everything was dumped to the floor whilst Reece bounded into the room.

"You motherfucker!" Reece repeated once more as his angry red face jumping over the bed and straight up head-butting Dustin. Stars flashed before him as an intense pain dug deep into his forehead. Not even being able to see, Dustin collapsed to the floor.

"Yeah!" said Reece with an air of triumph in his voice as Shawn and Jeremy stormed into the room, "That's what you get when you-"

That is as far as Reece got. Shawn threw a fist at his face, sending him straight into the emptied wardrobe. The wardrobe door cracked and splintered as he landed.

"Bring it!" yelled Jeremy, really beginning to get into the violence.

"Okay!" Reece yelled back, jumping up and pulling out his blade once more. Both Shawn and Jeremy's faces dropped. In all of the head crunching action, they had both completely forgotten about Reece's weapon in the space of literally a few minutes.

"Fuck!" Shawn and Jeremy fled the room as Reece bounded towards them both, knife in hand as he jumped over the unmade double bed.

Out upon the landing, the pair of them were just about to flee downstairs when they noticed Pesk at the top of the stairs. He had come round and it looked like Casper had done sweet fuck all about it.

"You'se gonna get it now famalam blud tings," Pesk coughed deliriously, his bloody head rolling upon his neck aimlessly as he struggled to keep himself balanced on his own two feet, "I'ma fuck you up!"

Shawn and Jeremy instantly went for the attic, hoping that there was some form of defence up there. Something that Robin had maybe hidden for his emergency weapon. Reece instantly chased after them but was kicked down by Jeremy as Shawn searched the room.

Seconds later, Shawn found what he was looking for.

"Fuck me," said Jeremy when he caught sight of what he had found, "Where the fuck did Robin get one of them from?"

"Where indeed..." Shawn pondered as he grabbed the machine gun from under the camp bed, "Maybe he swiped it from the museum in Crystalgate. Bloody convenient though-"

Shawn turned to find Jeremy had gone. Reece must have pulled him down the ladder. Clicking back what he assumed to be the safety, Shawn jumped down the ladder for a surprise attack.

And it really did come as a surprise. To everyone.

In his struggle with Jeremy, Reece had pushed him into Tommy's parent's room just as Shawn had landed. Without even being sure of what he was doing, Shawn pulled the trigger with devastating effect. Bullets flew everywhere as the gun bounced uncontrollably in Shawn's hands, each one popping out of the muzzle with an ear-tearing bang and eventually embedding itself into something with its own unique sound.

Reece bore the brunt of it initially, his body becoming a bullet-ridden sack and within moments he twitched and collapsed to the floor. As the gun continued to fight Shawn's loose grip, his aim turned to the rest of the landing, tearing the woodwork to shreds and finishing off Pesk with a stray shot to the head in the process. Finally, the roof took the last of the available bullets, plaster and bulb shards falling to the ruined carpet as they were violently pummelled with bits of speeding metal.

Silence followed when the magazine had run out. Breathing a huge sigh of impalpable relief as the last of the dust settled, Shawn placed the gun down. They had done it. Despite the odds, they had done it.

As Jeremy peered from a door riddled with bullet holes, Shawn calmly stared at the horrific mess before him. There was blood everywhere, bullet holes in every object; the stair banister totally disconnected from the wall and the plaster was still showering down slowly. His ears were ringing deafeningly in the silence that had followed. He noticed Pesk's body by the stairs, red bodily fluids oozing from the bullet holes. Who the fuck owned Gullum now?

"What a day it has been for us in 'Z-Land' today, thanks to Victoria for that name, she won the naming award yesterday so to hell with place names like Morrhead and Sinthwaite, everywhere is 'Z-Land' now," the ignoramus on Crapital FM blabbed in the background as Dustin pondered on his speculative question, *"Over to the news and other than an apparent sudden shortage of drugs that caused Amy Winehouse to die once again, the day was slow-"*

Dustin knew the answer. The I Shower Naked Club of course. And as the clock tower distantly rang five, he knew that it was time to skin up and prepare the next deal.

DAY 6

An important lesson had been learned from Robin's death and they all knew it. It was the next day and Dustin, Shawn, Jeremy and Casper were all sat round in Tommy's kitchen once again, contemplating their next move. Tommy's house still looked like it had been used as a set for a horror movie, the removal of the bodies of Robin and Pesk and his henchmen only adding to the trails of blood staining the carpets. It seemed as though they couldn't get enough of the red stuff.

"The problem is, we never expected other survivors to be an issue," said Dustin over another delicious portion of cold tinned food on yet another ridiculously sunny morning, "We went at it too loud, assuming we could just do this."

"Finally, someone talking sense at last!" Casper said, frowning with annoyance slightly, "Now let's pack this in!"

"Lolwut?"

"Why would we pack it in?" Shawn asked.

"Yeah, with that Pesk guy out of the way, we own Gullum," Jeremy replied, "We win!"

"We do win," Dustin confirmed, "Unless there is someone else, which there just well might be, we've won.

For now."

"Are you guys seriously going to continue with this dumb plan after all that has happened?" Casper moaned, "People have died for the fucks sake!"

"Indeed they have," Shawn smirked, his eyes glancing out to the Tommy's courtyard. A motionless Pesk was out there, chained up by the dog leash and collar he had left behind. None of Pesk's gang seemed to be considering a zombie afterlife.

Casper gawped as though he was lost for words.

"Look, Casper, you know that you have it easy don't you?" Jeremy asked, "All you have to do in return for survival is keep on top of some spreadsheets and stats."

"You call this survival?" Casper continued to moan, "You call these thugs trying to kill us is part of survival? Not only do we have zombies to worry about now, but fucking lunatics!"

"Pretty much," said Jeremy, who appeared to be enjoying whatever he had in his tin of food.

"What would you have us do?" Shawn asked.

"Sit around and hot-seat Total War or Civilization or something," Dustin replied.

"No, I'd have us doing something that would actually get us more food," Casper snapped back, "You guys do realise we're on the brink of running out, right?"

A short pause followed as Jeremy chewed on his food and the rest chewed on what Casper had just said.

"What do you mean?"

"We're getting just enough to keep us going," Casper said, "If we don't make deals everyday, we're going to end up running out."

"We'll make deals everyday then," Jeremy said with a full mouth.

"No we won't," Dustin replied, "Our clients are going to run out of supplies. Or the need for draws. We need a fresh supply of custom."

"Yo!" Shawn yo'd, looking somewhere between

confused and serious, "Fuck all that hype, I've just realised we have a car!"

"Wut?"

"Shit, he's right," said Dustin, mentally cursing that he'd forgotten about Pesk's car, "Did anyone grab the keys off that loon?"

"I put all his stuff in one of Tommy's boxes," Casper mumbled, not looking best pleased at the recent revelation, "Upstairs somewhere, probably the attic."

A dramatic pause filled with sound of mental activity was followed by a mad rush as everyone except Casper scrabbled to the attic in a mad race for the keys. Shawn was pushed down the stairs by Dustin in the chase, but it was Jeremy who managed to push ahead and rapidly ascend the ladder to the attic.

Once in the attic, Jeremy threw the shelf contents on the floor, hurriedly trying to find the keys before either Dustin or Shawn caught up.

"C'mon, c'mon, c'mon, where are they!?" he gritted his teeth as he sent books, comics, DVDs, ashtrays, figurines and numerous copies of FIFA flying across the room in his desperate bid to find the keys first.

Bombarded with airborne shelf items as he climbed into the attic, Dustin jumped straight at the shelf where Jeremy was searching, accidentally sending the entire shelf crashing down upon both of them.

"Fuck!" Dustin cursed under the shelf as a plastic globe bounced off his forehead and Jeremy struggled to slide from under the heavy wooden shelves.

By the time the pair of them had struggled out, Shawn had already arrived and found the box Casper had talked about. He stood there, amused as he watched Jeremy and Dustin's struggle whilst picking the keys out of the small Tupperware box that contained Pesk's personal junk.

"Slow and steady," grinned Shawn, pretty much jangling the keys in their faces.

Jeremy attempted to swipe the keys from Shawn's hand as he climbed up from the ground, unfortunately knocking the box out of his hands instead. Jeremy was showered in several permanent markers in varying colours, a couple of broken clippers, a draw of bud and another small button bag of white powder.

"All this fighting over the car keys is dumb anyway," said Dustin as he got up, taking the keys right off Shawn, "With Robin gone, I'm the only one here who can drive."

"Fuck off, you don't need a licence anymore," Jeremy snatched the keys off Dustin.

"Jeremy, have you ever driven before?" Shawn asked as they made their way downstairs.

"No, have you?"

"Yeah, my Dad's a driving instructor, remember?"

"Was a driving instructor."

"Fuck you, he could still be alive."

"Yeah, and Wil Layne could be a very talented man just coasting through life, but we all know what's more likely."

Pesk's red Ford Focus had remained untouched since the drug snorting sadist had parked up outside Tommy's house. The dead eyes of Pesk watched Shawn jump into the driver's seat as Dustin and Jeremy checked out the boot.

"Shit son," Dustin exclaimed as Jeremy and himself looked down upon a sandwich bag of MD that Pesk had collected, "I forgot about all of this."

"He must have liked tagging his name everywhere," said Jeremy, eyeing a bin liner that was bursting full of half used and spent spray paint cans of varying colours.

"Fuck that, we're sat on a goldmine here!" Dustin felt a pinch of the white power and crystals between his fingers, letting it drop back into the sandwich bag, "Looks to be at least twenty grams of the stuff in here!"

"You mad?" Jeremy looked at Dustin as though he had flipped, "Shifting draws is hard enough in this zombie age. Now you're wanting to sell some serious mind-altering stuff? Who's gonna buy it?"

It was a good question, one that Dustin didn't know the answer to. If only Pesk was still alive. Then they'd have a buyer.

Pesk's run down car coughed and spluttered for a few seconds before reluctantly being forced to start. The engine roared furiously, turning many indignant zombie heads in their direction.

"IT WORKS!" Shawn cheered, not really caring about the oncoming zombie horde.

"Sweet man!" Jeremy jumped into the passenger seat as Dustin picked up the bag of MD and carried it to the driver's side window.

"It's not all good though," Shawn spoke over the noise of the engine, "According to the fuel gauge we're running on fumes. Or the fuel gauge is broken."

"We'd better move guys or we're going to end up a Jill sandwich," said Dustin as he rapidly carried the sandwich bag of MD into the house.

Jeremy and Shawn looked around to find that Dustin was right. The zombies were now approaching from all directions, seemingly mesmerised by the chaotic noise of the Ford's decaying engine. Another twenty seconds and they'd be surrounded.

"Shit son!" Shawn cursed as he ripped the keys from the ignition and clambered out. The pair of them followed Dustin to the house and closed the door.

Casper must have switched on the radio as it was blabbing away in the background as the three of them peered through the gap in the curtain at the zombie horde milling around outside.

"Shit son," Shawn repeated as a horde of at least a thousand zombies swamped the area.

"What do we do?" Jeremy asked.

"Probably just going to have to wait for the clock tower to strike so they'll move on," Dustin replied, walking off to the kitchen.

"Fucks sake guys what have you done!?" a cry of annoyance from Casper floated from upstairs. Looked like he'd noticed.

"We have three hours to kill before the three o' clock bells then," said Shawn said, "Not that we need anything, are we all prepped for today's sale?"

"Did the bagging first thing," Dustin called from the kitchen door as he walked in with a drink of cold tea, "We're good to go I think."

"So what are we gonna do?" Casper asked as he bounded down the damaged stairs as though he was attempting to save himself from falling.

Several pairs of eyes switched to the Pesk's sack of MD sat on the kitchen table.

"Wait- NO!" Casper saw their eyes and intentions and reacted with horror, "You guise gotta be mad!"

After a moment's thought as Dustin rustled with the MD bag, Jeremy agreed with Casper.

"You're right," he said, his serious face defiantly on, "We'd be really fucking stupid if we were to-"

Jeremy was interrupted by a loud snorting sound. They glanced over to find Dustin snorting a key of the MD. He gazed back at them with a stunned look as the effects built up inside of him.

"Wot?" he asked, tweaking and sniffing as the other three stared at him with horror.

"You just-"

"Aw come on it was one key!" Dustin chatted fast as the MD energy built up inside him, "Ffffwwhhoa! Goddammit! This stuff is kinda intense!"

"Fucks sake," Casper grumbled as he grumpily slouched in a chair as though he was determined to be in a bad mood all day.

"C'mon fools, have a key," Dustin smiled manically in a way that probably wouldn't convince them as he sniffed about the room as though there was a peculiar smell in the air.

"Eh? Whaddya think?" Shawn asked Jeremy, both curiosity and boredom in his eyes.

Jeremy glanced at the wide-eyed Dustin who had started bopping slightly to the rubbish music pouring out of Crapital FM with enthusiasm despite some clear unease on his mind on what he was dancing to. It was clear Jeremy was not comfortable with the idea.

"I dunno…"

"C'mon, c'mon, c'mon," Dustin articulated with impatience, "Don't worry about it, I'm just happy. I'm not gonna jump out of the window or start killing fools or whatevs."

Shawn caved in.

"Fuck it," he said, arranging himself a line to snort, "We're gonna be bored shitless and we could die any day anyway. Want one Jeremy?"

Jeremy was still unsure. However, after watching Shawn take a bigger line than Dustin, he decided that hashtag-YOLO was a much more fun mentality to have during a zombie apocalypse and snorted a line, albeit messily, blowing white powder across the table.

"Ugh, snorting stuff is horrid," Jeremy squinted his eyes and pulled a face similar to that of when he was taking a shit as his body absorbed the drug.

"Yah might be better dropping it instead of snorting lines," Dustin bounced, his eyes beginning to resemble large shiny saucepans.

"'Yah' might be better sitting still," chuckled Shawn as he watched Dustin bounce into a shelf. Several of Tommy's family photos and a copy of Red Eyes and Rap Rhymes crashed to the floor thanks to Dustin's drug endued hyperactivity. And he wasn't alone. Both Shawn and Jeremy were beginning to bop along to the Crapital FM music that they'd usually regard as trash.

"Why don't we play some video games?" Casper suggested quietly, dreading the house being trashed by lunatics on drugs once again. With luck, Dustin had heard him.

"Yeman, vidya gamze!" he cheered, throwing his arms out as though he was doing star jumps, "Whadd we got?"

"Someone say vidya gamze?" Jeremy and Shawn's attention were suddenly on Dustin and Casper.

"We got FIFA-"

"FUCK FIFA!" Dustin roared, making poor Casper jump, "It's the same fucking game released for forty flitting pounds every year. Let's play a real game!"

"Total War it is then," Casper grinned, pulling out his laptop.

"Fuck dat!" this time it was Shawn who didn't like something, "I ain't ever told you guise this before but seriously, fuck that game too! Its so boring man!"

"Wuut!?" wutted Casper, shocked to hear his beloved game was being trash-talked.

"Yeman, wuut?" Jeremy pushed Shawn with friendly aggression, "Total War is the gamze of all gamze."

"Wouldn't go as far as the gamze of all gamze but its fucking better than FIFA," Dustin added, still bouncing about uncontrollably.

Despite this, Shawn put FIFA into Tommy's Xbone anyway and grabbed himself a pad as both Jeremy and Dustin continued their obsessive bopping.

"Yo, this stuff is pretty strong," Jeremy grinned at Dustin with pupils the size of planets within his eyeballs.

"Yeman it's some of the most pure MD I've had," Dustin replied as he danced to some awful pop tune uncontrollably, "Last time I was on this stuff I ended up chatting shit for hours man. No way you could stop me, I mean, literally, there was no stopping me. Words just kept on coming outta my mouth for some reason, I always had something to say. Yadda yadda yadda for hours and hours and hours. My cousin ended up shutting me in a cupboard I ended up talking so much it was crazy and even then, I didn't stop. Just kept on talking. Talking forever. Revealed my deepest and darkest stuff that night man, I swear, forreal! It was ridiculous really, I don't even know why it happened-"

"Dustin!" Shawn interrupted the drug influenced speech, "You're doing the exact same thing now fam! Shuddup or get in a cupboard! Now who wants to play FIFA with me?"

Nobody wanted to play FIFA with Shawn.

"Honestly, I'd rather eat glass," Jeremy laughed at his own joke loudly before dipping back into the bag of MD, "Man this stuff is real moreish."

"True dat!"

Casper meanwhile, was watching the chaos slowly unfold, his eyes wide from horror rather than drug abuse, clutching his precious laptop as though the outlandish behaviour he was witnessing would cause it to melt. Still the only sober one out of the four, he declared upon deaf ears he was going upstairs to play some Total War.

Outside, the ocean of zombies droned past without much care, the bright and hot sunlight pummelling UV rays into their dead organs.

"Yo," Dustin yo'd, "Do ya reckon zombies get sunburnt?"

"Nah," replied Jeremy as Shawn uttered a 'yes' at the same time. The pair glanced at each other, surprised that they'd both answered different things at the same time and turned back to Dustin to reply the opposite of what they first said.

"You don't fucking know do ya?" Dustin snapped, chuckling inside at their cluelessness.

The pair shook their heads and returned their gaze back at the television.

"Well, I'ma have another line, you guise in?"

"Yeman," they both replied, still bopping to the music but also transfixed upon the game of FIFA Shawn was having at the same time.

"Roll a spliff as well fam," Jeremy added.

"No, you fucking roll a spliff," Dustin shot back, "I'm preparing lines blud."

"Oh ye."

Spliff rolling and line making took longer than expected. In fact, Dustin was surprised to find an entire hour had slipped by them since he had last announced he was prepping lines. His mind boggled over it as Jeremy rolled three spliffs.

Outside, the horde of rotten corpses was still flowing thick and fast, the summer sun beating down heat decay upon them as they grunted and snarled past Tommy's house. Whilst rolling his spliffs, Jeremy noticed that the living room curtains were still open and a handful of the undead were making weak efforts to break in.

"Fucking gross!" he exclaimed, spliff in mouth as he closed the curtains, hiding the decomposing pained expressions from view.

His head spinning with drugs, four by four beats and euphoria, Dustin crashed down next to Shawn and attempted to figure what was going on in the virtual football match.

"I can't see shit, yo!" Dustin finally said after scrutinising the television for about a minute, "I just... can't focus on it."

"Chillax mah breadbin," Jeremy slouched on the back of the sofa, passing Dustin a spliff, "Shawn yo, dat game nearly done fam cos ya got a line and a bud."

"Dunno," Shawn replied, fighting with the controller as his glassy eyes bore into the TV screen, "I don't think I've even set up a game yet."

Jeremy squinted at the screen but was unable to come up with anything to say. Not that there was a silence. The rubbish pop music was still blasting out of a low quality radio speaker and Dustin had begun talking once again. The three continued taking drugs and talking mostly nonsense, occasionally attempting to get a game of FIFA going when they realised they were still on the game's main menu. Time passed in a way the three never really expected. It had practically melted away like Salvador's pocket watches. Fast.

"Today we've seen the resurrection of Melson Nandela which has brought great joy to Z-Land. May we all remember his 'I dreamed a dream' speech with muchos respectos, and maybe after all this time the dream he dreamed has finally become a reality. Meanwhile Twatter is down, as is every website actually, probably because we've been posting more Twats than ever, hold tight, I'm sure it'll be back up..."

Dustin found himself upstairs with Casper in the attic. It was past six, the three o clock bells hadn't done anything to distract the horde away and neither had the six o'clock ones. With re-animated dead bodies still flowing thick and fast, now banging furiously on the windows and doors of Tommy's house, perhaps something to do with Jeremy turning up Crapital FM, they were forced to cancel the day's sales. Nobody was able to pick up whilst the zombies were at large outside.

Casper's craptop's battery was on the brink of dying since he had left the reach of the generator. He was using the last of his juice to check his spreadsheets as Dustin chatted away and blew weed smoke at him.

"-and I know you won't appreciate this idea, but me and Shawn-"

"Shawn and I," Casper the grammar Nazi interrupted.

"-whatever, Shawn and I were really thinking about repeat custom. Cos we know we have competitors now, there's probably someone who was doing what we were doing like Pesk was doing if ya get me. Someone in Lower Gullum or Puddock could be at it right now, stealing our customers 'n' shit so we were thinking rewards system or the occasional free draw we could work out for tomorrow-"

"Free weed?" Casper frowned, "I dunno if you noticed but we're only just scraping by as it-"

"-which is exactly why we need to get some loyalty!"

Dustin exclaimed excitedly as though the idea was literally the best thing since sliced bread, "Think about it! We need to make sure that our customers know that we are there for them, that we're not there to milk them dry-"

"-Dustin!" Casper pointed Dustin's eyes right at his spreadsheet, "Look at the numbers okay! We can't really do this unless you fancy going a few days without meals."

A confused Dustin stared at Casper's craptop blankly, toking his spliff and dropping ash on the campbed. He could make out the bright white of the screen but not the important bits that Casper was referring to. His eyes were a drug addled blur.

"Are you even listening?" Casper demanded, less than impressed with Dustin's lack of real response, "This is what I was telling you all this morning, before you fell in love with a car and a bag of drugs! We have literally got food for today, that is it! We've been living day by day and it doesn't help that Jeremy never sticks to the ration plan and just eats what he wants when he wants. Not to mention Moonface has yet to pay up for any of the weed he's bought-"

"What!?" Dustin was alarmed at the mention of Moonface, he stared a Casper with an intense scowl, his giant eyeballs glittering with anger, "What about Moonface!?"

"He hasn't paid us Dustin," Casper replied calmly, relenting his frustration now Dustin had started to take matters seriously, "He owes us ten tins of food, not counting what he probably wants to tick from us today."

Dustin was silent for a moment. He jumped off the campbed and began pacing the attic as though he was attempting to contain an explosion within himself.

"Goddammit. That motherfucker," he breathed as Casper nervously watched him pace, "That MOTHERFUCKER! That fucking little moonface'd prick!"

"Calm down-"

"CALM DOWN!?" Dustin roared louder than he had ever done before, now pacing faster than ever, "That little fucking cocksucker fucked me before the apocalypse, and now he's still fucking me after it! And you expect me to calm down!?"

"Dustin-"

"I'ma rip his head off and shout into the bloody remains of his fucking neck!" Dustin literally jumped down from the attic through the ladder hole, landing in the hallway of the second floor heavily.

Nobody from downstairs questioned what the noise was as Dustin strode furiously down to the living room as though his rage was feeding off the sound of FIFA. Casper was left alone in the attic.

Jeremy and Shawn were slouched on the sofa, completely succumbed to a haze of weed smoke, MD crystals and video games, totally ignorant to the zombie apocalypse outside and Dustin's drug fuelled temper storming in like a crackhead on vengeance. Neither of the pair had a chance to react before Dustin had screamed his way into the room, lifted the TV above his head and threw it at the living room door. Glass smashed.

"What the fuck!?" Shawn stared at Dustin as though he had just taken a dump in his breakfast.

"Fuck you Dustin, FIFA isn't as bad as you say," Jeremy jumped to his feet.

"Fuck me?" Dustin seemed confused, "Fuck Moonface! That cunt owes us food and we're running out!"

"Y'wot?"

"You heard," Dustin fumed, pacing once again as Jeremy and Shawn let the message sink into their distorted minds as the TV continued to spark and splutter, "He's screwing us! He's screwing us and taking us for fucking fools!"

"How much?" Shawn's face had darkened in expression as Jeremy continued to grin helplessly.

"Still tho Dustin, why the TV?" Jeremy was still shocked over Dustin's entrance.

"How much?" Shawn grabbed Dustin and glared at him with entirely black eyeballs.

"Five draws," Dustin shouted at Shawn's face, "That slimy fucker owes us ten tins of food at least!"

Shawn marched straight for the door, "Jeremy! We're off to go show Moonface what happens when ya fuck with us!"

Dustin grabbed the car keys as Jeremy grabbed one of the BB Guns and Shawn equipped himself with the golf club. Ignoring the fact that the street outside was completely teeming with the undead, the three ploughed their way to the car as quickly as they could. Dustin jammed the car key into the eye of one stood in front of the driver's seat floor as Jeremy fired BB pellets into their air as though he was on some sort of movie bank heist.

"Phew," sighed Shawn one they were all safely in the vehicle.

"H-hey, I've still got a spliff," Dustin said was amazement, surprised to find a smoking spliff in his hand as the zombies outside began to rock the car.

"And I've still got our MD, so what?" Jeremy stuck his face into the huge sandwich bag of white crystals.

"Drive motherfucker!"

The blood soaked key didn't want to start the engine initially, but Dustin forced it. The engine spluttered to life once more and Dustin accelerated straight into the zombies and then eventually the abandoned wreck of car in front of him.

"Fuck!"

Crunching gears, Dustin reversed, doing the exact same but backwards, jolting them all in their seats as though they were trapped in one of them fake rollercoasters.

"Goddammit!"

"Dustin! They're gonna get in, get us to Street D!"

Third time lucky. Dustin managed to both accelerate and turn at the same time, avoiding the cars and lampposts peppered about the street. The zombies however, were crushed under the wheels of Pesk's car. As they sped up towards the end of the street, the sound of bone-crunching upon tarmac subsided as the zombie numbers thinned.

"Hey you guise," Dustin said, out of breath for some reason as he smoked his spliff, "I can't see shit man. Why am I even driving?"

"Cos we're gonna fuck Moonface up innit blud," Jeremy bounced in his seat, the white powder built up around his nostrils dropping into his lap in snowflake sized clumps.

"Fuck."

Dustin took a sharp right turn, totally missing the turn in the road and instead performing a swooping curve straight into someone's garden face. Good job the residents of Gullum had little pride over their properties. The rotten fence smashed and scattered all over the pavement as Dustin continued to steer, narrowly avoiding the solid looking hedge that guarded the garden of the next house.

The car rocked as Dustin dumped it back onto the road, once again running straight into a zombie. Bones snapped and a gaunt looking zombie face was now somehow stuck on the bonnet, gurning and grinning at Dustin like the drugged up fools sat behind him as he blindly raced through the dirty streets of Gullum.

"Oi! What we gonna do when we get there?" Shawn asked, doing his best to ignore Dustin's terrible driving.

"This world is as big as our oyster," Jeremy replied, his head in the MD bag once again.

"Save some for the rest of us poomplex," Dustin said, jealous mirror eyes watching Jeremy snort key after key of the MD.

Shawn grabbed the bag off Jeremy and helped himself to some more, "We've smashed this stuff pretty fast ya'know blud."

"Fuck off," was Dustin's response as he diverted his attention from driving to grabbing the bag of MD, "If I'd wanted comeback I'd have got it off your mum's face-"

"SHIT!"

Dustin narrowly avoided an oncoming car. Fighting over the drugs had taken his attention off the road and he had very nearly crashed straight into a fellow driver. He swerved out of the way at the last minute as the second working car in Gullum blared it's horn angrily at them. Right at the moment when he swerved, Dustin noticed what car it was. It was the grey Renault Clio that Pesk had almost hit the day previous.

Losing control, Dustin simply gave up with attempting to drive as the car screeched round and round until it ploughed straight into a building on Street D. There was a bang and a showering of white powder. A few stone bricks clattered on the bonnet as the building crumbled. The windscreen had shattered and smoke was beginning to pour out of the car's bonnet. The zombie head that had been stuck upon the bonnet had flown straight into Jeremy's lap.

"What the junk man?" Jeremy seemed cross as he lobbed the zombie head out of the car, "Man's dropped the MD."

"Fuck!"

"Who was that guy?" Shawn was still staring at the road behind them through the shattered back window as zombies began to take interest in them and gather round.

"Right now I don't give a fuck," said Dustin, jumping out and not even attempting to get the smoking wreck of a car back running.

"Yo famalam help man grab all this MD up," Jeremy was bent down, trying scrape the ruined powder off the car's floor.

Without a word, Shawn grabbed Jeremy and pulled him out of the car, Jeremy protesting loudly as he did so.

The zombies had nearly surrounded them and the wreckage of Pesk's car. Giggling slightly from the high of the drugs and the sheer absurdity of their situation, Dustin pushed Shawn and Jeremy down Street D towards where Moonface had been squatting.

"Fucks sake guys," Jeremy continued to moan about the loss of drugs.

"Shuddup Jeremy there's enough of the stuff on your sleeve to fuel a house party," Shawn gasped as they sprinted for their lives down the black street.

Behind them, the zombies had picked up their pace to a run. Screaming at the top of their partially decomposed voices, they chased the three drugged up fools hungrily, casting haunting silhouettes in the dying light of the day.

Despite the seriousness of their situation, Dustin was unable to feel much panic. His vision and emotions were padded away by a large soapy bubble. Or a room full of cushions. His mind was unable to focus upon one thing and he found he had to keep reminding himself that they were off to Moonface's and they were being chased by zombies. Why were they being chased? Didn't they have a car?

Jeremy nearly ran past the house where Moonface had been living. Shawn's outstretched arm grabbed onto the hood of his hoodie and pulled him towards the wooden door. Dustin was surprised how quickly they had sprinted down the street. His heart was threatening to jump into his mouth.

Shawn slammed into the door. The lock gave instantly, the door swung open with enough force to kill a man.

"Hands on balls, bums on walls!" Jeremy yelled, firing the BB gun as he strode into the darkness of the living room, "The I Shower Naked Club is here motherfucker!"

"Fucking hell, bit keen," Dustin muttered, following the pair inside. The zombies chasing them didn't seem to notice they had turned into a house and raced straight past, taking their sickening sounds with them.

Moonface's living room was in darkness. In fact, the entire house was in darkness. It took a moment for Dustin's tuppence sized pupils quickly adjusted to the darkness.

The house had clearly been stripped bare. Stripped bare and decorated lavishly with rotten body parts and stale blood. The foul smell crept up their noses like a contagious death. Jeremy gipped at the sight of something gross.

"Aw fucking hell man!" he wailed, his hands with the BB Gun on his head, "There's a mashed up corpse here."

"Y'what?"

"It's got bullet holes and bite marks and guts everywhere," Jeremy despaired as though the sight was the most horrible thing he'd seen, "What a mess, it's horrible, it's like the grossest thing I've ever seen- oh wait it's just some old blanket never mind."

"Baghead."

The kitchen was just as bare as the living room. Even the cupboard doors had been stripped, vacant holes where utility draws should have been. The smell of rotting wood, blood and stale smoke continued to creep into their lungs. There was a long and sorry looking kitchen table that had certainly seen better days, probably days when it propped up family meals instead of post apocalyptic wastemen who went by the name of 'Moonface.'

There he was, in all his orbital glory. Slouched at the end of the nearly broken table, he appeared to be scraping out a weed grinder with a large screwdriver. He looked up and seemed pleased to see them.

"Safe guys, you dropping off draws now since the zombies were out all day?" he beamed. His beam didn't last long.

"POW!" Jeremy roared, laying a heavy punch straight into Moonface's moon-like face. Knuckle came in contact with nose. Knuckle won. Moonface's nose buckled and the sheer force of Jeremy's punch sent him twisting round backwards, falling of his chair and plopping on the floor like an oversized rag doll.

Despite successfully knocking Moonface out in one clean 'pow,' Jeremy seemed concerned at his own actions. He immediately inspected Moonface's unconscious body with worry.

"Shit, he okay?" he asked Shawn and Dustin with worry in his eyes. Both of his peers immediately began laughing.

"Oh, wow, how much sniff have you taken?" Dustin beamed, before glancing around in a confused manor as though he'd lost something, "Where even is it?"

"You crashed the car dickhead," Shawn pointed out as Jeremy attempted to shake some life into Moonface.

"Oh ye..."

"Guys, I think I've killed him," Jeremy panicked, repetitively picking up and dropping Moonface's limp arm.

"Good," said Shawn who had begun searching the kitchen, "Man this guy has fuck all. I don't think he was ever going to pay us back."

"Not surprised," Dustin said flatly, staring at Jeremy freaking out over the immobile Moonface, "We shoulda never trusted the cunt."

"True talk," Shawn muttered, still scanning the place, "I'ma search upstairs, you two dispose of that twat's body."

"I don't think he's actually dead y'know," said Dustin, turning to face Shawn, only to find he had disappeared already.

Dustin looked at Jeremy and Moonface for a moment. Jeremy still seemed paranoid over Moonface's unconsciousness. He had started jabbing him furiously in the face in some bizarre attempt to wake him up.

"Jeremy," Dustin said pulling his arms to stop him from poking the moon, "Let's just shove this guy outside and let him get eat, innit?"

Jeremy appeared really confused at Dustin's

suggestion. He began panting heavily like a marathon winning dog. Dustin slapped him across the face.

"Dafuq?" Jeremy was really angry at being slapped. Grabbing the bright orange BB gun, he tried to bring it swinging down on Dustin's face. Dustin quickly dodged Jeremy's attack and Jeremy ended up just swinging at thin air.

Dazed over the sheer energy he put into his failed pistol whip, Jeremy spent a moment of time confused at what just happened. Dustin shot an intense stare at him, debating mentally whether he should attack and wondering what the hell was even happening. His vision and mind was clouded and a conclusion was never made. He didn't want to fight Jeremy, he just wanted to be friends.

Jeremy however saw things in a different light. Very confused and wondering where on Earth Shawn had gone, he was angry. He didn't even know why. Did everyone else know something he didn't? Was he the butt of some kind of joke? Why did he feel like everyone was laughing behind his back? He wasn't fucking laughing that was for sure.

Jeremy launched himself at Dustin again, slamming him up against the wall where a fridge may have once lived.

"Whoa, whoa, whoa, whoa, what the fuck?" Dustin pushed Jeremy away, "Get the fuck off me!"

"One vee one me bro," Jeremy growled, his fight slowly becoming a joke as he realised what he was doing, "Right here, right now."

"MLG bitch! Wanna take it to the curb if you can stand it?" spat Dustin, still giving Jeremy evils, unsure if he was going to attack again or if he had finally snapped out of his rage.

Jeremy laughed. And then began crying.

Dustin was lost for words. He stared blankly at Jeremy who was sobbing next to Moonface's body. What on Earth had just happened?

"Sup mate?" Dustin put a friendly arm on Jeremy's

upset back, still unsure if Jeremy was in the mood for raging. He'd have normally guessed not, but having seen his mood change three times in the blink of an eye, Dustin was still cautious.

"I think my mum's dead!" Jeremy wailed out of the blue.

"I think so too," Dustin's attempted sympathy fell flat, "Now let's get rid of this moon faced prick innit."

Dustin pulled Moonface up off the chair. Jeremy begrudgingly helped, wiping tears from his eyes. Together they dragged him across the kitchen door. Fortunately the back garden door was unlocked and they were able to dump him on the paving outside.

The garden was small, bleak and basking in the evening's moonlight. A scruffy and balding lawn in front of a path of cracked paving flags, all surrounded by a chest high stone wall that appeared high enough to keep the zombies out, for now. At the opposite end was a gate leading out to Street C.

"Right, let's open that gate," muttered Dustin walking towards it. A sniffle from Jeremy behind him made him pause, "You okay mate?"

Jeremy sniffed loudly, "I don't think I can do this mate. I can't kill him."

Dustin cursed mentally. Four damn contrasting emotions in four crazy minutes. Jeremy really was a trip.

Then, to make matters worse, Moonface began to come round. He stirred, letting out a high pitched groan as though he'd just orgasmed without stimulation.

"Shit," Dustin marched back to the two without even knowing why.

"Guise?" Moonface peeked up at them both. Without thinking, Dustin snatched the BB Gun off Jeremy's limp grip and pointed it straight at Moonface.

"Don't you fucking move!" Dustin spat, panting and sweating, hoping Moonface wouldn't attempt to escape.

Fortunately, Moonface appeared to fear the toy being

pointed at his head, remaining deathly silent and perfectly still, his black pupils reflecting a full moon each. Dustin peered closer. The reflections of the moon in his eyes looked like they had a face on it. Moonface's face. Instead of checking the actual moon in the sky above him, Dustin peered closer once again. Sure enough, Moonface's face was on the moon. Trippy.

"What are you doing?" Moonface breathed, frozen in fear at the sight of Dustin peering closer and closer into his eyes. It looked like Dustin was approaching for a kiss or something.

Realising how stupid his little tripping episode was, Dustin felt foolish and a spark of embarrassed rage inside him made him slap Moonface around his planetary head. Dustin stood up to find Jeremy looking at him strange.

"What?"

"I-I can't do this Dustin," Jeremy looked paler than both the Moon and it's distant-relative-face.

Dustin looked at Moonface, who was still on the ground. Despite having great feelings of animosity, he knew he couldn't bring himself to kill him either.

"Me neither," Dustin threw the BB Gun down on the ground, "But this little fuckwit his crossed us too many times! Think of all the times he fucked us about!"

"Think of all the times I let you guys chill at my yard," Moonface's high-pitched raspy voice polluted the air.

"True, this guy is a friend," Jeremy smiled, laughing with some relief, "We should let him join the club, not kill him. Especially since we don't have Robin anymore, we could use the extra hands"

Dustin said nothing. He was certain there was a reason why they wanted to kill Moonface, but right now, his mind couldn't come up with anything. Why on Earth had they ever acted so aggressive to him in the first place? A conclusion was never made. There was only one thing for it. Moonface had to stay.

"Get up!" Dustin still seemed to be acting aggressive

despite letting Moonface in the group. Something was still bothering inside him, but with a clouded mind, he couldn't fathom it.

Moonface stood up, passing over the BB Gun back to Dustin.

"Safe!" Dustin yelled, offering a fist to bump. The pair awkwardly fist bumped, Moonface's moon face clearly unsure about everything.

"Yeman safe!" Jeremy beamed, despite still acting aggressive towards Moonface, "Welcome to the 'I Shower Naked Club.'"

"T-thanks man..." Moonface attempted a smile, but was clearly still shaken up and unsure of the situation.

The three of them were about to return back to the house when Shawn burst out, clutching quite impressive dagger, it's taper twinkling in the bright moonlight as the noise of zombies droned on in the background like an oppressed vacuum cleaner.

"Yo famalams, guess what I've found," his cheer stopped abruptly when he noticed Moonface was still alive, "Dafuq guise? We were meant to be killing his faggot arse, not taking him out for some air!"

And with that Shawn threw his newly acquired knife at Moonface's face. A flash of spinning chrome landed straight into Moonface's endless, pale forehead. The tip of the blade poked out the other side. Black blood began to dribble down his face like ooze trying to escape a sore. He stumbled and stuttered in confusion as his body figured out what had occurred as both Jeremy and Dustin looked on, their horrified expressions forever etched onto the memories of Moonface's last sight.

He collapsed to the floor loudly, letting out another pained wail that could quite have easily been mistaken for pleasure. In the cold silvery light of the full moon, Moonface slowly and silently died, his black blood seeping into cracks of the paving as he twitched uncontrollably.

Both Jeremy and Dustin were lost of words. They both

stared at Shawn, speechless.

"What? He was a cunt, he stole our weed," said Shawn, scowling at the vacant expressions on the pair's faces.

"Oh, yeah," Dustin's mind slowly re-realised what all this was for. He glanced at Jeremy. It seemed he was thinking pretty much the same thing.

"He's like a penny, two faced and worthless," Shawn continued to justify his actions, not that he felt he had to, he just felt he'd stumbled into an alternate universe where they were out to befriend Moonface.

Dustin realised his head was sore. The warm ball of goodness inside him was fading, and the need to impress and socialise and dance was fading. His mind couldn't even begin to make sense of anything. He began to feel emotionless and cold. And wide awake.

"Let's go home," he said, completely forgetting there was a bleeding Moonface behind him.

And so the three of them trudged home. The zombie plague had pretty much cleared up in Upper Gullum by this point, and their journey back to Tommy's house was much less eventful than their last journey. What was perhaps most disturbing for Dustin was that he was still seeing Moonface's face in the night's full moon. He was shining down upon them, the sheer sight of him irritating Dustin once again. He'd somehow reach space and have Shawn stab him again if he could. Hopefully a bedtime spliff would stop the hallucinations.

DAY 7

Casper, as per usual, hadn't been impressed at Shawn, Jeremy and Dustin's little trip. He had spent the time in their absence worrying, not that he could do much else. Fuel for Total War video games and spreadsheets had run dry and with rations running low due to the day's deal being cancelled, Casper's time had mostly been spent watching the zombie numbers slowly thin out as the night progressed and worrying about what could have possibly happened to the rest of his group.

However, that wasn't all. They had a visitor.

"Hello there lads," Tommy's bearded face poked out of the front door as the three of them returned from their adventure to the moon, his winter woolly hat bobble bouncing like an excitable creature on the top of his head.

Dustin wasn't sure if he was still tripping or not. It was still very dark and he'd been seeing glowing worms on all the zombies he had killed on the way.

"Hey look, Tommy is here!" Jeremy seemed to cheer, reassuring Dustin that he wasn't tripping.

"Oh gawd," Shawn breathed as they stepped into the house.

Something clicked in Tommy's hand as they walked

in. The silvery light of the moon shining through the crack of the door revealed the silvery gun in his hand. This was the second time Dustin had faced a gun since the apocalypse began. The first time hadn't really worried him, but with the deadly look in Tommy's eyes, the three of them knew instantly that he wasn't happy with them. Even if the MD stopped it from really sinking in.

"In," Tommy snarled, flicking the gun towards the kitchen where Casper was. The three of them silently joined Casper next to the kitchen table.

There was a nasty silence. Casper was too terrified to speak and the other three were too drugged up to even figure out what the deal was. Tommy was pissed off, but at what was a mystery. Dustin was the first to have a stab at what was up.

"Look, Tommy, I'm sorry we took your house and grow but-"

"Shuddup!" Tommy yelled, his voice echoing down the hall and silencing Dustin who just stared at him with bafflement, "You think you can just jack my stuff, betray my man and leave here walking?"

"It'd be nice-"

"Shuddup!" Tommy yelled once again. Another nasty silence.

"Betray your man?" Shawn asked after a lengthy moment of sheer nothingness.

"I sent my man Joshua up here," Tommy growled, moonlight twinkling in his eyes in the monochrome atmosphere, "And you man jacked him, thinking I was dead or something! Are you stupid!? Do you think I'm stupid!? 'Cos I'd like to think, you don't think, that I'm stupid, you get me?"

Both Casper and Jeremy were frozen in fear, Jeremy's huge black pupils having taken over his entirety of his eyes. Shawn was just stood next to them, looking neither afraid nor confident. He just looked confused. Dustin felt the same. He couldn't even focus on what Tommy had just said. Forcing events to replay in his mind, Dustin sat down, sighing as Casper began to nervously play with the empty fuel barrel.

"Problem fam?" the gun was pointed at Dustin, but with his mind in his current drugged up state, he couldn't fathom the sheer gravitas the situation was intended to have.

"We never saw Joshua," he lied, rubbing his eyes in hope it would help his blurred vision, "He wasn't here when we arrived and he hasn't come since. We didn't even plan to stay here, the first plan was to go to Carpathian Mills but when we checked that place out it was... too dangerous. Since then, we've been shifting your grow to survive, we didn't know you were still alive."

Tommy peered into the vast eternal void that was Dustin's eyes. After a moment he shook his head, relaxing, "What the fuck is wrong with you guys? Your eyes look fucked and you're acting like kids who know they're in trouble."

"It's complicated, we were threatened by this Pesk guy and we ended up killing him and taking all of his MD," Dustin sighed once again. His brain was mashed.

"Then Dustin crashed his car and I think we've just killed Moonface because he owed us and couldn't pay," Jeremy continued.

"And now we're here," Shawn finished the story. Casper remained silent.

Tommy looked at them with a mixture disbelief and amusement, "You killed Pesk? And you ticked to Moonface? Who's idiotic idea was that? I wouldn't even tick him before we had this zombie problem. He's a wasteman."

"He's wasted man," Shawn grinned.

Tommy didn't smile back. His eyes told a story of deep distrust. The gun was still firmly grasped in his hand. Something didn't make sense in Dustin's mind, but he couldn't figure out what. His mind was only focused on how everything was black and white. Like some old movie. Crazy.

"What happened to my sofa?" was Tommy's next question. This time, Casper replied.

"Robin died on it."

"Yer fuckin' wot? Robin was here too?"

"Pesk killed him."

"And what happened to my TV?"

"Dustin smashed it up when he was on MD."

Using his gun hand, Tommy rubbed his forehead. He shook his head with disbelief, "So let me get this straight. You come here, start ticking my grow to that Moonface cunt, get Robin killed, kill one of the biggest drug lunatics in Morrhead, take all of his sniff and crash his car before killing Moonface?"

"Pretty much."

Still struggling to believe their tale, Tommy refocused the barrel of the gun towards the direction of the three of them, "And throughout all of this you didn't see Joshua once?"

Dustin shook his head, "Nope.exe."

Tommy sat down. He discarded the gun upon the table. The colour seemed to return to the world. Dustin, Shawn and Jeremy seemed surprised to discover the sun was rising already.

"S-so you're not going to kill us?" Dustin asked, still wide eyed.

"No point really," Tommy shook his head and took his beanie hat off revealing his scruffy, matted hair, "It isn't as if it's your fault Joshua didn't make it here. And it sounds like you guys have had a rough ride here anyway. You sure it was Pesk you killed? That man is next level."

"Deffo him, he's chained up outside," Casper nodded, not smiling, "He was gonna take over our crappy plan."

"How many times Casper?" Jeremy elbowed him with annoyance, "This plan is the best."

"And what plan is that?" Tommy asked, "Sell my

grow for food I guess?"

"Pretty much," Dustin repeated.

"Where does Casper fit in all this?"

"Spreadsheets."

"Would be spreadsheets if we had any fuel," Casper said, bitterness heavy in his tone, throwing the blue barrel at the wall. It bounced off and knocked over a free chair.

"We're out of fuel already?" Jeremy sighed, "How have you used that entire barrel already?"

"It burns fast!" Casper protested.

"It will do when all you do is play Total War," Shawn pointed out.

"True you want to be playing some FIFA there lad," Tommy said, "I'm sure I had a disc somewhere-"

"So where does that leave us?" Dustin interrupted to avoid a discussion about FIFA as Jeremy randomly turned to face the window and began slowly moving his right hand fingers up and down in front of his eyes, "You must have come here with your own plan, right?"

Tommy scratched his beard, glancing at Jeremy who was still looking at his own fingers move in front of his face as though he was playing an imaginary trumpet, "Was the same plan as yours. Just with Joshua. Who isn't here. So yeah, you guys can stay but I'm on this since it's my bud and yard."

Dustin internally breathed a sigh of relief. For a moment it looked like Tommy would be angry enough to kill them and they'd have another Pesk situation on their hands. He wouldn't put it past him. Always friendly to them who were buying, but never suffered the fools who messed with him.

Jeremy turned from the window, a scowl of hurt and betrayal on his face, "Fuck the Queen," he grumbled.

"Ya fuckin' what lad?" Tommy asked.

"She didn't like my song," he stormed out of the kitchen, slamming the door behind so hard that some of the stained glass the frame held within fell out and shattered on the floor. Silence was maintained as they all heard him stomp upstairs and into one of the bedrooms like a child having a temper tantrum.

"He's probably still tripping," Shawn grinned nervously, "He went a bit mental with the sniff whilst driving to Moonface's."

Fortunately, Tommy didn't seem fazed at Jeremy breaking more of his house.

"At least we have a fresh gun now," said Dustin, eyeing up Tommy's pistol and putting a pre-rolled spliff in his mouth.

"Oh, that ain't a gun lad," Tommy replied, throwing it at Dustin who only just managed to catch it, "It's one of them fancy cigarette lighters."

Dustin lit his spliff with the gun-lighter, staring at Tommy inquisitively.

Unsurprisingly, Tommy had insisted on having his bed back, despite Jeremy being KO'd on it. This meant someone had to be demoted back to the sofa and it was looking like it might be Casper, much to his horror.

Dustin had been feeling emotionally hollow all morning, unable to come up with any feeling. His mind was clouded and he was just witnessing events as they happened, like he was a fly on the wall. He'd been mood-hoovered. Staring at Tommy, Shawn and Casper debate at the top of the stairs whilst Jeremy snored loudly.

"I want my camp bed," said Casper when he realised he was going to lose the camp bed, "I'm not going back on that sofa."

Their minds thought of the horrific mess that had been on the sofa since Robin died. Screw that.

"Your camp bed lad?" Tommy smiled, "Everything in this house is mine."

"Jeremy can sleep with me in your parent's room," Shawn said, rubbing his vacant eyes as though he was just about to drop off to sleep.

"I'm having the camp bed, go fuck yourself Casper,"

Dustin droned, blinking and not looking at anyone.

"Well where can I go then?" Casper seemed appalled, almost on the verge of tears.

"Jump on the ceiling if you want," Tommy grinned, finding Casper's misfortune amusing.

"Plenty of space up there," Shawn smirked, "You'll have the room to yourself."

"Your very own lamp too," Dustin joined in the piss-taking, pointing at the single bulb dangling off the end of a grubby wire.

"Go fuck yourselves guys," Casper trudged back downstairs in a sulk, stomping his feet so loud that the zombies outside fruitlessly made their way to the front door and began their pathetic fist slams.

"Nice one dickhead," Tommy stormed into his bedroom and began ousting Jeremy off his bed.

That left Shawn and Dustin, alone on the landing, listening to nothing but the disturbing sound dead hands clawing at the front door. They were both defiantly coming down from the MD.

Shawn was first to speak, "I don't even..." he began, unable to finish his sentence.

"Me neither," Dustin was still staring at the ground, unable to feel much inside. Events had changed dramatically and yet his mind was unable to process it correctly.

Shawn stared at Dustin blankly. So much had happened, they had so much to discuss, and yet neither of them could find any of the words needed to express themselves. They just stared at each other sympathetically.

"We need to make sure he doesn't find out about Joshua," Dustin finally whispered, glancing over to Tommy's bedroom nervously.

Shawn nodded and also glanced around sheepishly, "I doubt he'll find out unless one of us mess up."

"Casper basically," Dustin nodded, looking grim and paler than ever.

Shawn said nothing. The pair of them, wide-awake and yet feeling dead to the world. They were practically zombies. The pair of them watched the zombies bang at the door fruitlessly for a while, not even feeling any sense of excitement or danger. They were blank canvases. Without an artist to work on them. And maybe the canvas was imaginary.

*

It had taken two hours for Dustin to get some sleep. And even then, he was only gone for an hour before he was disturbed. Tommy was in the attic with him, bagging up for the day's deals.

"I thought this was your job lad," he said, carefully weighing out dried buds on the set of scales that were most likely inaccurate.

Dustin squinted. The summer sunshine was pouring through the attic window. It felt like he was trapped in a greenhouse. His head hurt and his mouth was dry. The world felt like ashes. He said nothing and just sat up on the camp bed.

"I'm taking over shotting," Tommy continued, still weighing out draws. Dustin remained silent and grabbed himself a pre-rolled spliff, using Tommy's fake gun to light it.

Nothing but the oppressive moaning of dead people from outside, the light crinkling of button bags and the cracking of burning herb could be heard. Dustin inhaled and exhaled loudly. A smile of relief crept on his face.

"It's weird you know," Tommy began picking leaves off the plant for drying, "You man was the last I was expecting to survive. Back when it first broke out, I was shopping with Joshua at Didl, the one up by Fortress Mound. We thought we had a solid plan nailed down. But I was... unlucky, ended up being stuck at the Carpathian Mills. You see lad, they have these barrels of unused oil round the back I figured would be good to refuel my car since it works with diesel cars. Plan was simple. Joshy lad would head straight through Puddock and to my yard to secure it, I would refuel my car and join him when I could. Then we would... I dunno. Probably sell draws like you guys. I just wanted to find my family really."

Dustin stared at Tommy for a moment. Tommy had no idea he was being stared at; he had his back to Dustin.

"What happened?" Dustin asked, taking a huge burn on his spliff picking up a nearby hardback copy of Nineteen Eighty 420 in an appearance to look more relaxed and causal.

"Y'wot?"

"Uh, what, erm, happened? To you at the Carpathian?" Dustin blinked nervously. He knew Tommy was a sly motherfucker and was not expecting him to be okay about everything that had happened. Even if he claimed he was.

"My car was robbed and the fuel I had prepared taken too," Tommy hung his head in a defeatist manner, "I fucked up lad. On the way I decided to follow Duke to the Cow's Face, that pub at the top of Sinthwaite. Said he had some gear to pick up and he'd sort me out if I helped. I gave him a lift and the fucker just abandoned me when he found his shitty wreck of a car. I was a day behind by the time I reached Carpathian. Then a set of raiders took my shit. Car, fuel, the lot."

Breathing heavily and taking another burn of his spliff, Dustin stood up. He didn't know whether to leave or not. He didn't know what would look more suspicious. He didn't even know if Tommy had suspicions.

"Any idea who they were?" he asked whilst Tommy continued bagging up.

Tommy inhaled sharply, shaking his head, "No idea lad. They're probably dead by now. If not, I'll kill the fuckers myself."

Dustin had no idea how Tommy expected to do that

when he had no idea who they were.

"How about you lad?" Tommy looked up at Dustin with burden-heavy eyes that looked forever sleepless, "Carpathian Mills? You went there right?"

"Not for long," Dustin looked away, unable to lie whist looking at Tommy, "Didn't even get through the car park- wait!"

Dustin turned to Tommy. Something wasn't right. Dustin had done the bagging up the day previous whilst off his tits on class A drugs. Why was Tommy bagging up now? The orders hadn't changed since their previous deal had to be cancelled.

As though he had read Dustin's mind, Tommy gave an explanation, "We have a new deal, my man Dany wants six draws."

"R-right, does Casper know about this because he'll want to note it down his notepad of dictatorship," Dustin blew out thick and heavy smoke that danced its way upwards to the attic roof.

"Yeman, told him this morning after he told me your showering naked plan or whatever."

Almost going wide-eyed for a moment, Dustin considered what Casper may have already told Tommy. Had he already contradicted their story? What had Casper told him?

"I'm assuming you're sorting it out after the first deal?" Dustin stood up and slipped on a t-shirt.

"Assume?" Tommy picked up a discarded FIFA case and a sharpie pen and wrote the word ASSUME on it in large black letters, "Assume makes an ass out of you and me lad."

He drew two lines, one between the second S and U and a second between the U and M. ASS|U|ME.

"More of an ass out of you in this case though lad."
"So…"

"Casper agreed to do it," Tommy replied, dropping the FIFA case and taking the smoking spliff out of

Dustin's mouth.

"Ya-fuckin-wot? You managed to convince Casper to do something? How did you manage that?"

"What can I say lad?" Tommy continued to smoke Dustin's spliff as he returned to his bagging up, "I can be convincing sometimes, innit."

Dustin wasn't convinced. Unsure if it was still the effect of the MD that was causing this unease, he trudged down to the kitchen to get some food. If they had any left that is. He hadn't eaten in what seemed like forever and now his stomach was feeling funny.

He found a Shawn, a half eaten tin of chicken soup and a radio on the brink of running out of battery, all sat in the kitchen idly.

"But one of the real questions of the day has to be, has the z-land become more sexist since the zombie revolution? Well, let's ask this dumb slag we found-" the one and only radio station, Crapital FM, continued its post-apocalyptic pollution of the radio waves.

Shawn looked up at Dustin. His eyes looked heavy.

"You eating that?" Dustin pointed at the chicken soup as he slumped in a chair.

"Nah," Shawn blinked, "Can't eat, it's like swallowing needles. And Casper is insisting on rations until we do the two deals we have today."

Not caring about Casper or rations and nearly knocking over the radio, Dustin grabbed the soup. Unlike Shawn, he was ravenous. The cold soup brought some relief to his taste buds and stomach, making them realise once again that life was actually probably worth living. Maybe.

"Where's Jeremy?" Dustin said as he munched on a mouthful of soup. He sprayed the kitchen table with his gob.

"Still asleep I think," Shawn continued to stare. He still looked totally out of it, completely oblivious to the world. Dustin found a smile creeping to his lips. The continued vacancy of Shawn's personality was somewhat amusing.

"Have you even slept?"

"Nah. Dunno how Jeremy has managed it."

Dustin thought back to his pitiful three hours in bed and nodded his head in agreement.

Together they sat in silence a while, before Dustin broke the potentially bad news.

"Tommy was at Carpathian you know."

"Yeah, he mentioned it-"

"We took his fuel and his car."

"Oh," Shawn stared at the table for a moment, "So… not only did we send Joshua away to die, but also we fucked up Tommy's plan by taking his stuff. Fucking great! Does he know?"

"Don't think so," muttered Dustin, keeping his voice and head low, "We just need to make sure there is nothing here to contradict our story."

"Which is?"

"We attempted to get to Carpathian, but it was too dangerous."

"That was the best you could come up with, yo?" Shawn seemed irritated at Dustin's cover story.

"You try coming up with a story on the spot," Dustin screwed his face and rubbed his forehead which was beginning to pound, "It's intense. It's like hitting yourself with a brick. Anyway, it should be fine! There is nothing here that says otherwise."

Shawn nodded his head in agreement and the silence returned with nothing but the ignorant jabber of the radio to be heard. Then it clicked. Both Dustin and Shawn looked up at one another with alarm. There was something that contradicted their story.

Dustin saw the look in Shawn's eyes as realisation dawned. Together they both turned to look at the blue empty fuel barrel that Casper had been tossing around earlier. Empty, upturned and very blue, it was in the corner of the kitchen, punching a huge hole in Dustin's story.

"Maybe he didn't notice," Shawn hoped as Dustin attempted to do some social equations in his mind.

"We're... going to have to assume he didn't," Dustin said finally, standing up and grabbing the barrel, "We need to get rid of this. You good to spot if I find somewhere to throw this?"

"Yeman."

"C'mon then, quicktime before he comes down," Dustin hurried to the front door. There were still a few zombies making pathetic attempts to kick the door down. Shawn grabbed a machete that belonged to either of them goons who worked for Pesk and joined Dustin at the door.

"On three," Dustin breathed, grabbing the door handle as Shawn made sure he had a firm grip on his weapon, "One... two... three!"

Dustin pulled the door open and they were both greeted with a zombie each. Swinging the barrel, Dustin literally took the head off the zombie in front of him, which was so rotten it was already threatening to fall off under the pressure of gravity alone. The body collapsed as the head was sent spinning across the garden like an out of control cabbage.

Shawn sent the blade straight into the depths of the second zombie's neck, nearly detaching it's head as well. Realising his blade was stuck in rotten flesh and bone, he kicked the zombie away, freeing it from his blade. Stumbling backwards, the un-dead sack of rotting matter continued stumbling until it finally tripped itself backwards over Tommy's garden fence, landing on the zombie-ridden pavement with a dry crunch.

"Yo, these things are actually rotting away," Dustin said, fascinated as he strode out into the garden, "They're becoming more of a danger to themselves than they are to us."

"Yeah but they seem more aggressive. C'mon brah, throw that thing somewhere so we can get back inside."

Dustin spotted a lone wheelie bin across the road. The zombie activity was picking up, but not too much to handle. Choosing his moment well, Dustin sprinted across the road, nimbly avoiding several swipes from the zombies that were milling around. He dropped the barrel in the bin and then jogged back.

"That looked close," said Shawn, "You need to be more careful- hey- look!"

Dustin turned to find what Shawn was pointing at. It was a zombie, but not any old zombie. It was Shawn's waste-of-skin brother, Jack, still clearly being a waste-of-skin as he groaned and walked with the rest of the un-dead army. The most amazing thing however was that he was carrying his Blu-Ray player, the cable and plug dancing behind him as it bounced off the ground whilst he walked.

"Heh, wut?" Dustin couldn't find the words.

Jack groaned on past, still gripping his Blu-Ray player as though his non-existent life depended on it.

"You okay?" Dustin turned to Shawn who was still staring at his dead brother walk past.

"Yeman," Shawn found a smile to his face, but he was clearly lost for words.

With their incriminating evidence hidden away, the pair watched Jack stumble into the descending afternoon sun and off into the depths of Upper Gullum.

*

Before they knew it, the evening had arrived. With two deals to execute, the days haul was expected to be good. Surprisingly, it was Casper who had stepped up to explain how things were going to go down.

"Okay, I've decided that Jeremy and Shawn will do the usual deal on Street D whilst Tommy and myself sort out Dany's draws at the clock tower," he said, showing off one of his rare moments of decisiveness whilst stood on top of Tommy's kitchen table, "Then we rendezvous back here, hopefully without having to kill anybody alive or mess up Tommy's house anymore than it already is."

It seemed Casper's main prerogative was to cut out anymore violence. Dustin found his words refreshing over their chaotic day of drugs and violence, however he noticed one thing he had issue with.

"What do I do?" he asked, noticing his name hadn't been mentioned.

"You're growing and quality assurance, right lad?" Tommy grinned, "You stay here, make sure everything goes smoothly."

"And what if it doesn't?" Dustin scowled back immediately, "Sure, we have a laser system for Street C, not that it did Robin much good. But the clock tower? I'm not sure if that's the right place-"

"That's where we're meeting Dany, like it or not lad," Tommy put his foot down.

Noticing Tommy and Casper glance at each other, Dustin wondered if a secret agenda had been planned between the two. He forced such destructive thoughts out of his head. If he continued being paranoid of everyone, he'd no doubt end up attempting to kill everyone in their group.

"One more thing," Tommy sneered as he put on his winter themed woolly hat, "The I Shower Naked Club is a rubbish name. I'd prefer: 'The X-Rated Gangster Niggers.'"

"But none of us are black..." Jeremy muttered as both Casper and Tommy left the room. Looked like they were commencing the deal procedure.

Dustin, Shawn and Jeremy all glanced at each other, confirming their feeling of unease at the sudden power shift.

"C'mon! Let's go and make this cushdy!" Tommy swung the front door open, helping himself to a machete and walking out. Shawn and Casper followed, grabbing a weapon each and leaving Dustin and Jeremy in the house.

"I'm right tho, right?" Jeremy turned to Dustin, "We're not black! We can't say that word, innit! We're not x-rated either..."

Dustin remained silent, watching the three jog down the street through the window as they sliced up and battered many rouge zombies on the way.

"I mean, I know Tommy isn't racist like, I know it's just a joke, but other people may not see it that way! It might hurt sales, people might misunderstand. We can't let him change the name fam, I Shower Naked for life! Are you okay?"

Dustin was still staring out of the window, his frown still painted on his gaunt face.

"Fam?"

Without warning, Dustin grabbed the last machete and kicked open the door, totally destroying the rotten door frame which fell out and broke on the garden paving with a loud clatter.

"Dafuq?" Jeremy found himself surprised at Dustin's seemingly spontaneous actions.

"Look!" Dustin pointed at the street. There were roughly a dozen zombies droning about the street, several of them dragging themselves across the ground with bony and decomposed limbs. Jeremy focused on what he was pointing out. It wasn't good news.

Joshua was stumbling down the street, looking very, very dead. He had white and vacant eyes coupled with a huge maggot-filled gash running down his neck, and his head wobbled and struggled to keep balance; all of which told a story of how one man was rejected from the I Shower Naked Club and tossed back into a cruel zombie infested world.

"Well shit," Jeremy said, "Guess he didn't survive."

Dustin looked at Jeremy, still wearing the same frown, "Goddammit! Don't you remember anything about yesterday? Tommy was going to kill us over this! Or so it seemed anyway..."

Jeremy looked at the ground, confusion on his face whilst he shook his head. He had no idea what had occurred the day previous.

"Well fuck," Dustin spat on the ground, "Tommy probably knows we're lying if that cunt is still walking about Gullum! Why couldn't he die in fucking Sinthwaite or Puddock or some other miserable village in Morrhead?"

The zombies on the street, Joshua especially, were beginning to take an interest in Tommy's open door. They had seconds before they were to be overrun.

"I don't like this at all," Dustin said, prepping the blade in his hand, "Hold the fort fam!"

And with that, Dustin sprinted out of the door and took off Joshua's head with the blade, sending black blood and rotten flesh spraying across the street. Poor Jeremy was left at the broken door, waiting for Shawn's signal and feeling slightly helpless.

Avoiding as many swipes from the re-animated dead as he could, Dustin ran down the street as fast as his legs could take him, dangerously and blindly swinging and thrashing the blade about as he ran. Diverting off the street, Dustin hurtled down a snicket between the house rows down to Street B and along to the end where the clock tower was.

The clock tower, Gullum's grey obelisk, stretched upwards with row after row of stone brick, as though attempting to escape the miserably lousy village and join the sun where things were undoubtedly warmer and brighter. The clock face glowed softly in the dying light of the day, boldly telling the alive and un-dead residents of Gullum it was quarter to six.

Wiping blood from his eyes, Dustin approached the clock tower that appeared to be mostly devoid of zombies. There he found Tommy, Casper and a blonde person who must have been 'Dany' just in front of the tower, seemingly just talking in the stone paved square that sat at the base of the tower.

Approaching the three quietly, Dustin bent down to find cover behind a particularly thorny bush next to the peeling entrance railings. Tommy seemed somewhat enraged.

"NO FAM!" he roared at Casper, grabbing his t-shirt and pulling him close to the blade in his hand, "I'll tell you exactly what this deal is lad, I'm taking my yard back!"

With that said, Tommy quietly and slowly slid the machete into Casper's chest. Casper gasped in shock, his face twisted into a look of pain, shock and distress as blood spilled from his mouth and sprayed across Tommy's face.

In the vast orange light of the dying sun, Casper slid to his knees, still choking on blood as he did so. A shaking, blood-soaked hand outstretched as though Casper was asking for pity from his killer. Or maybe it was mercy. Or maybe he had noticed Dustin approach. Either way Casper finally ran out of air and slid backwards off Tommy's blade, sprawling on the ground in his final moments of horrible consciousness, blood seeping out from behind him, stretching across the ground and seeping into the cracks between the paving stone as though the very life from him was attempting to escape his body.

Casper was dead. Very dead. He wasn't coming back.

Shocked at what he had just witnessed, Dustin knew that he should remain in cover and not let his anger get the better of him.

But it was too late. He found himself hurtling towards Tommy with the second machete, wondering what on Earth he was attempting to accomplish with starting a fight he'd most certainly lose. Sure enough, brothers of steel clashed as Tommy instantly recognised Dustin's attack and countered it effectively, sending his blade flying out of his sweaty grip and clattering on the stone paving next to a pool of Casper's blood.

Seemingly amused, this 'Dany' character kicked the back of Dustin's knees, laughing loudly as he fell to the ground with a pained grunt. Within a few violent seconds, Dustin was at Tommy's mercy, staring at him from the ground and the wrong end of a machete.

Tommy looked Dustin right in the eye for a moment before he started laughing with Dany. Dustin considered making a move whilst they were both chortling loudly, but thought better of it. Why had he even attempted to attack anyway? It wasn't as if Casper was even that much of a valuable member of the club. It had been a foolish move.

"Foolish move lad," Tommy chucked, confirming Dustin's thoughts, "I ain't as green as I am zombie looking."

"Wot?"

Tommy grinned with clear excitement as he enjoyed the moment of power he had over Dustin, waving the blade around in front of him tauntingly.

"You think we don't know what happened to our Joshua?" Dany asked, also grinning, peering over Dustin's head.

"Well, yeah I do know you know... that's why I'm here," Dustin replied, shifting his back on the ground slightly as though he was attempting to get comfortable.

"No lad," Tommy laughed, pulling something long from his pockets, "You're here because I planned it."

Dustin had to squint through the dying light of the day to see what Tommy was holding. After a moment he realised. It was Pesk's dog collar and chain. The very same they had taken after it had been used to kill Robin. He must have used it to get zombie Joshua back onto Street A.

"You already knew..." Dustin whispered, his mind catching up with the events being played out before him, "This was a trap. You knew all along we had sent Joshua away."

"Damn fucking right I fucking knew!" Tommy roared, with little care for his surroundings or how many zombies he attracted, "You think you can just take man's shit and just get away with it?"

"Yeah…" Dustin nodded, finding the question amusing. For some reason it reminded him of when he was locked up at Pesk's. A smile found its way to his lips.

Tommy stepped back, a look of bitter fury in his eyes, "This ends now," he uttered, spitting on the ground. He raised his machete for the kill. If Dustin was to move, it had to be that very instant.

Dustin didn't move. He was paralysed in fear and this was most certainly the end. And it would have been if something hadn't distracted Tommy.

"Whass that smell?" he look a large sniff of the gentle evening breeze, his face turning even more bitter. Dustin took a smell himself. He knew that distinct pong. He had smelt it pretty much every day post zombie apocalypse. It was the raw and crude smell of rotting people.

Tommy glanced behind him to find about half a dozen zombies charging into the courtyard of Gullum's clock tower. If there was a chance for Dustin's escape, it was now.

Rolling over, before either Tommy or Dany could react, Dustin scrabbled up and dashed straight for the clock tower. Glancing around and cursing loudly, Tommy followed, chasing straight after Dustin, clearly hoping Dany would defend against the zombies. Dany did nothing of the sort. Grabbing Dustin's machete, Dany sprinted in the opposite direction from the zombies, parkouring straight over the iron fence that surrounded the courtyard and out of sight behind a patch of trees.

Not even sure what he was thinking, Dustin grabbed the nearest corner of the clock tower's exterior and began frantically climbing the brickwork upwards away from Tommy and the un-dead. To his horror however, Tommy followed, climbing straight up the clock tower after Dustin.

Noticing his assailant climbing desperately after him, Dustin attempted to pick up the pace, relying on the decadent design of the stonework for foot-holes and places to grab. He was rapidly reaching the middle of the clock face and it began to dawn on him how high he actually was. Both metaphorically and literally.

Looking down, Dustin noticed two things. One was that Tommy had diverted off Dustin's climbing route, opting to shimmy along a ledge under the clock face, away from the corner Dustin was climbing. Amazingly, he was climbing with the machete in his mouth.

The second thing was that even some of the zombies had attempted to climb. Most failed to get anywhere, not having the strength to pull themselves up. But one had made it up about three or four foot and Dustin looked down just in time to see it's brittle shoulder joint to fail and break, sending it falling to a bone-crunching second-death. The bony hand continued to cling onto side of the tower.

Basking in the orange light of the nearly dead day, Dustin found himself at the top of the clock tower, hanging for dear life onto a single spire that lavishly crowned the top of the clock tower as Tommy began to make his way up the clock face. He had grabbed onto the minute hand that was pointing at ten to six and was seemed surprised that his weight hadn't made it give. If Dustin didn't do something quickly, Tommy would reach the top.

Realising Dustin would be stuck at the top, Tommy took a breather as he precariously balanced himself in-between the hour and minute hand, flashing a victorious grin upwards.

"End of the line lad," Tommy laughed, now holding the machete, "You've nowhere to fucking go! You're trapped!"

"So are you!" Dustin called back, not sounding quite as confident as Tommy did as he hugged the top of the clock tower. He didn't want to admit it, but he wasn't very good with heights.

Tommy stopped laughing but continued grinning. It

wasn't a nice grin. It was bitter and filled with evil intent.

"Brilliant," Tommy smiled disturbingly, steadying the blade in his hand, "We can truly get to know one another lad. Because all I really know about you is that you like my weed and you don't like FIFA."

"You don't know shit about me!"

"I know, that's what I've just said!"

Tommy began his climb up towards Dustin. Dustin looked down. It was either face Tommy or face the collection of zombies on the ground, numbers of which had easily doubled with many more gormless dead faces staggering into the courtyard. Several had already started tucking into Casper's carcass. Yet again, he had to act and he had to do it quickly.

Nothing could figure out what inspired Dustin's next move. It was both really stupid and really brave at the same time. Knowing that death was almost upon him, he knew he had no choice but to take one massive risk to save his skin. With a fierce battle cry, he leaped off the top off the clock tower, aiming straight for Tommy. Amazingly, his feet landed on the minute hand that Tommy was grabbed onto, which immediately gave under the weight of two people and swung down to half past.

For a sickening second, Dustin thought he was a goner, doomed to falling into the horde of zombies below, however a lucky outstretched hand flailing about in desperation managed to grab a hold of the very end of the minute hand that was now pointing directly at six.

A strange clicking sound came from within the clock face. Looking up, Dustin attempted to work out what was going on, but he need not have. The clock tower began its automated half-past chimes, the bells so deafeningly loud, Dustin nearly let go of the minute hand. It was then he realised he felt unusually heavy.

Tommy's fate had briefly slipped his mind. It took a moment for him to realise where he had gone. An angry swipe from the machete below him revealed the answer.

Tommy was hanging into Dustin's ankle with nothing else but a large fall below him.

The bells of Gullum's clock tower worked its magic on lulling the zombies towards them. The un-dead flooded through the courtyard gates, mesmerised, as though they were following the pied piper.

Dustin kicked his legs in an effort to get Tommy to let go. Unfortunately this didn't help as Tommy's grip remained firm. Swinging the machete with desperation, Tommy took a swing at Dustin's back. Unfortunately, with all the moving and thrashing about, Tommy hit Dustin's ankle.

The pain was unbearable, like being struck by lightning. His vision blurred as his lungs let out a scream of pain through clenched teeth. Panic stricken, Tommy took a second swing. This time Dustin's bone snapped, causing him to howl in agony and slip down the minute hand a little as Tommy's weight alone tore the remaining flesh straight from the rest of his leg as the metal of the minute hand dung into the flesh of his fingers.

Dustin didn't even notice that it had been the very ankle Tommy had been hanging onto he had chopped off. Tommy fell straight to the ground with Dustin's foot and a good side portion of his leg, straight into a mosh pit of zombies. Either the fall or the teeth and claws of the zombies killed him, Dustin had no clue.

Taking a deep breath and forcing himself to keep a hold of the clock hand despite blood pouring from his fresh stump like a red waterfall, Dustin let out another moan of agony. He couldn't hear, he couldn't see, he could just feel. And it bloody hurt.

"Fuck, fuck, fuck, fuck, fuck, fuck, fuck!" he cried out, stifling his voice as he repeatedly hit his head against the minute hand as though he was attempting to distract himself from the pain, tears pouring from his eyes as he breathed heavily in an attempt to absorb the pain.

Darkness was approaching and with the noise of the

clock and the taste of fresh blood spraying upon their faces, the zombies were not inclined to move on. Dustin hung onto half past six, hoping to some unknown God that either Jeremy or Shawn would come to retrieve him.

It'd take more than a spliff to fix this mess.

DAY 8

Dustin stared at a hollow pit of nothingness. He was floating above an abyss of blackness. Or was he falling? Maybe it was more like gliding? He didn't know, but it sure was peaceful as he gracefully hovered. He could easily spend the rest of eternity here. How did he even get there? Neither the question nor the answer came to mind. Content in mind and spirit, Dustin drifted into the abyss, the void, the darkness, whatever it was.

Much to his despair however, reality began to appear, like an unwanted light at the end of a tunnel. It crept closer, bringing unwanted memories and thoughts with it. Before he knew it, Dustin was right on top of reality, his mind filled with pain and bitterness.

"Oh fuck."

A split second later, he was in Tommy's bathtub, surrounded by bright white light and the most vivid, almost fluorescent, red blood. The blood was quite literally everywhere, on the walls, in the tub, on the floor and covering Jeremy and Shawn who were stood in front of him, intense expressions of shock and dread engraved into their pale faces.

A second split second later, the pain kicked in,

booting into action, an invisible foot of flame avenging its lost brother. Fighting back tears of agony, Dustin looked down at the damage. But due to a plastic bag, that had probably once been white, with one of Pesk's dog chains strapped tightly around the wound, there wasn't much to be seen.

Emotions swirled within his insides as his mind made an effort throughout the pain to process what had occurred. Everything from the ankle below felt alien, as though it was just never meant to be. A strange itchiness to a pulsating throbbing ache to a sheer scream of agony was all felt at once. Each one taking a turn at the forefront of Dustin's attention, as though somebody somewhere had a mix desk in complete control of what pain he felt and was mixing hard to make sure Dustin felt the best of it.

"All hail the lecture brew…" Dustin passed out with the pain, sliding down in the bath of his own blood a little and leaving Jeremy and Shawn alone once again.

The next time Dustin found himself conscious, he was sprawled out upon Tommy's sofa. He coughed heavily, noticing the bed of dried blood he was resting upon. He couldn't tell if it was his own blood or the blood of the late Robin. Looking down, he saw his foot, stump, whatever was there, was still wrapped tightly in plastic and chains. It still hurt. Not the sharp pains of before however, just the unrelenting itchiness and the dull throbbing that felt like an army of antibodies were beating the shit out of everything in the area.

Dustin laid there, his mind racing and yet unable to focus on one idea. Simple thoughts bounced back and fourth like a dog chasing a tyre on a rope. Events hadn't quite sunk in. Casper was dead. Tommy was dead. He may as well have been too. One foot was bad news in a zombie apocalypse.

"YO!" he yo'd, hoping to get the attention of either Jeremy or Shawn. Silence replied. A worrying prospect entered his mind. Had Jeremy and Shawn abandoned him?

"YO!" he repeated to what seemed like nobody. Fury growing inside him, Dustin decided it was time to move. He rolled off the disgusting sofa and splattered on the lino flooring, his chest taking a heavy pound as he landed which made him cough once more. Now it was time to crawl.

Despite feeling weak, Dustin pulled himself along the floor, taking deep breaths as he did so. Fortunately the living room door was ajar, meaning there was no need for him to reach for the handle. He pulled himself through to the hallway.

There was a voice, somewhere, yammering away. He recognised it, but couldn't put a name on it. After a moment of catching his breath, he realised the voice was pouring from the kitchen. It was time to investigate. The more he got closer, the more he could make out the words.

"Zombie apocalypse getting you down? Need a helping hand to get back onto your feet? Too bad because nobody is here to help you. Nobody except the amazing, handsome and hardworking presenters of Crapital FM. They may not be able to literally help, but we can sure as hell sympathise. Or at least pretend to sympathise!"

Crapital FM. Dustin sighed. Of all the radio stations to survive the apocalypse, it had to be that mass polluter of the airwaves. He considered just laying in the kitchen doorway a while, but the ignorant jabbering of Crapital FM made him want to fuck the radio up. He was angry and confused and he had to take it out on something.

"Here at Crapital, we understand the confusion. We understand your anger. We understand you've probably been abandoned by your friends and family. We understand you were probably not very much fun to be with anyway. So here's some Wil Layne to sooth the pain."

"FUCK WIL LAYNE!" Dustin roared throwing an empty jam jar that was nearby at the radio. Amazingly, his aim was dead on, taking out the radio. Both items flew across the table and onto the floor, shattering to pieces upon impact.

"Yo, fuck you!" a familiar voice replied. The head of Jeremy poked around the corner, staring at Dustin with disbelief.

"No, fuck you," Dustin replied, smiling with relief as he gasped for breath. He hadn't been abandoned.

"Dude you look like shit," Shawn's head popped into view, looking concerned.

"No, you look like shit," Dustin's smile grew. His paranoia had gotten the best of him. He'd blame it on the weed, but he hadn't had any since the day previous.

Jeremy pulled out the Didl shopping trolley that they had been using to shot the weed in, "We can't have you dragging yourself on the ground, everyone will think you're a zombie. This will do until we find a wheelchair or something."

Dustin looked at the trolley. Undoubtedly something he would be unable to control himself, but at least it'd save his legs.

"I'd prefer a prosthetic foot over a wheelchair," said Dustin as both Shawn and Jeremy hoisted him up into the trolley, "What the junk happened guise?"

Both Jeremy and Shawn shifted uncomfortably.

"What?"

"W-we don't know," said Jeremy, casting a sympathetic look upon Dustin, "You ran off, we did the deal, had to listen to all them potheads moan that we didn't show up the day before and then we found you at the clock tower. You were lucky, you were passed out but the zombies were too busy eating Tommy and Casper."

"Yeah, we dragged you back here and checked you for bites," Shawn continued, "Other than a missing foot and a lot of blood loss, you seemed alright. So we left you and waited for Wil Layne's new track to drop."

"Yer-fuckin-wot?" Dustin looked as though he had just been slapped in the face as he pulled himself upright in the trolley, taking care not to disturb his mess of a wound,

"Wil Layne? He can't rap, since when have you guys rated his so-called music?"

"I know, but he's a zombie now, he's probably improved," Jeremy replied.

"True."

A silence fell between the three, only the squelching and groaning from the zombies outside to be heard. They all looked at one another with the same eyes. Tried and worn out eyes. Eyes that would be happy to close for an eternal sleep. They had lasted a week and what had they got to show for it? Nothing but trouble, death and competing dealers. It had been a hell of a week.

"So..." Dustin broke the awkward silence, but left his word hanging so another awkward silence occurred, "What are we gonna do?"

"Could smoke this spliff," said Shawn, pulling out a fat roll.

"Good idea yo," Jeremy agreed, helping himself to a handful of cookies, finishing off the remainder of the packet.

Dustin had an idea as Shawn sparked up.

"Where's Casper's craptop?" he asked, ignoring the plume of smoke escaping from Shawn's mouth.

"Over'ere," Jeremy slurred his words as he unexpectedly threw the craptop at Dustin, who only just managed to catch it, the force of the throw sending his trolley backwards a little at it crash landed into his stomach, "We got no power tho, so whatever battery it has left is all we have."

Dustin tried the power switch. The craptop failed to even recognise somebody was trying to switch it on. Casper had well and truly flattened the battery.

"Great," sighed Dustin, throwing the craptop to the kitchen floor, the force of the landing cracking one of the tiles, "Looks like he thought conquering Rome was more important than our stats. How much food do we have?"

"Well, we have that stuff over there," Jeremy pointed

to a small collection of tins on the worktop, whilst still chewing on his generous helping of cookies.

The small collection of tins in question really was a small collection. About five small tins of the most unappetising food Dustin had ever heard of. Prunes in vegan custard, Didl brand beef flavoured meat and a tinned quiche on which someone had scrawled 'I DIED HAPPY NOT EATING THIS.' No wonder Jeremy had taken the cookies whilst he still could.

"Have we got a deal today? Has Tommy even left us with any bud?" Dustin continued to quiz their situation.

"He took all of the supply, but we still have the plants left," replied Shawn, pulling out the sheet of orders and passing it to Dustin, "Guessing he was planning on taking it all after he killed Casper. Or something. I dunno. I'm not sure what went wrong to be honest."

Dustin looked at the order sheet. Orders were most defiantly down, only four draws requested, but at least that was something.

"He figured out we fucked up his plans at the Carpathian. And we turned away Joshua. He knew all along from start. It was all a trap," Dustin rubbed his leg with both hands, absorbing the pain from his hurting stump.

"You okay?" Shawn glanced over a copy of A Game of Tokes he was reading, noticing Dustin was still looking very pale.

"No," Dustin pulled a pained expression, breathing heavily, "I need some pain killers."

"Here ya go," Shawn passed over the spliff to Dustin. It was hardly co-codamol, but it would have to do. At least they didn't have to listen Casper moaning anymore.

"Do you think he was right?" Dustin asked out of the blue after a lengthy silence.

"Who?"

"Casper," Dustin continued, passing the spliff over to Jeremy, "He was always moaning that our idea was rubbish and to be fair to him, I'm beginning to think he was right."

"Meh," Jeremy meh'd, "I reckon that's the missing foot talking. Swimming with sharks is great until you get your foot bitten off."

"Y'wot?"

"What he's sayin' is that he thinks you're only thinking that now because you've had your foot chopped off," replied Shawn as he played around with a lump of tack he'd found under the table, "Let's face it. The man didn't engage, he had no ideas, he'd have spent the rest of his days playing Rome Total War in that shithole of a room of his until he'd have wasted away if we hadn't found him."

"True... but still though..."

"Still though what?" Shawn demanded, "We're still alive. The plan is still working. Let's not forget it was your idea all along Dustin."

Shawn was right, it had been Dustin's idea all along. He hung his head low, thinking of how they had spent a week in Gullum being well in over their heads, fighting drug crazed lunatics and then becoming the drug crazed lunatics themselves. Looking sorrowfully at his hurting stump, he couldn't help wondering if he had made the wrong call.

And it was there in Tommy's kitchen the remainder of the so-called 'I Shower Naked Club' spent the rest of their pre-deal time. With no power, no radio and a dwindling supply of food, all the three of them could really do was smoke their own supply. What little fun the zombie apocalypse had provided, had long since gone. It seemed like the people still alive were the most dangerous. Other than the occasional disruption and chase, the zombies had been a weak enemy in comparison to Pesk, Tommy and their various allies. Unless there was an overwhelming number of the undead fuckers. Then there would be a problem.

Six 'o' clock approached fast once again. At quarter to, Shawn set off to conduct the deal. Yet again, the sunset was huge and orange in a clear sky. There wasn't even a breeze. Gullum had probably never seen such calm weather.

Zombie activity was conveniently low. It seemed the disturbance at the clock tower the previous day had dragged the sorry animated corpses elsewhere, leaving the streets with just a handful of desolate faces grunting their way aimlessly down the tarmac arteries of Upper Gullum.

Street C was quieter than ever. Three potheads stood waiting at the lamppost and a few chopped up bodies scattered about the street. They were all holding blood-soaked makeshift weapons. Picking up drugs was a dangerous game during the apocalypse. Shawn recognised two of them, beanie hat dude and beard guy were back for their usual draw and there was one other person Shawn had yet to meet. One matter was concerning him however. There were only three people. He was expecting four.

"Yo, where's whatshisface?" Shawn asked as he approached.

"He's down there," Beanie hat dude replied in his monotonous stoned voice as though syllables were mountains that had to be climbed as he pointed to several pieces of corpse down the street, as the sound of a lone speeding car cut through the atmospheric silence, "He tried eating us, so we killed him, innit."

"Great," sighed Shawn, pulling out the green laser pen, "Let's get this over with then."

Shawn was just about to shine the all clear down the carousel mirrors when a grey Renault Clio screeched to a halt at the end of Street C, performing an impressive handbrake turn that span the car around to face them in a screeching symphony of worn out suspension and tired tires. There was a nasty silence as the four of them stared at the Renault in confusion.

"Who's that?" the new guy asked. Nobody knew.

The driver wasn't to be seen. Blacked out windows made it look like it was a transformer that had beef against them. Shawn knew it wasn't a transformer. He'd seen the car before, but he couldn't place where.

In another squeal of smoking tires, the Renault began speeding towards them.

"Ged outta here!" Shawn yelled, pulling out the red laser pen and sprinting for the carousel mirror. He had to get the message back that he was being attacked. Not that Dustin would be much use, but Jeremy would be.

The potheads scattered, each one sprinting out of sight with their pitiful so-called weapons as the car span to a halt once again. A small Asian man with a oblongish head stepped out, wearing a tight grey t-shirt, black jeans and reflective shades, he immediately walked over to Shawn who was fumbling with the laser pens.

Shawn failed getting the message out as the bloke grabbed him by the chest and pinned him up against the wall.

"Evening fam!" he grinned, showing off several gold teeth as Shawn finally got a good look at his attacker.

The shock of who it was nearly winded him. Another pre-apocalypse dealer known only as 'That Guy' was grinning right at him.

"Seriously?" Shawn sighed.

"You man have been busy!" That Guy grinned as Shawn stared into his own scared reflection from That Guy's lenses, "I recall the days when you yewts used to pick up from me!"

"You mean like, last week?" Shawn replied, tensing as he noticed the un-dead had begun to take an interest in their commotion, "What do you want?"

That Guy relaxed for a moment, easing his grip on Shawn as he looked back at his question with amusement, "What do you think?" he chucked as though it was obvious.

Shawn saw his chance. He swung a right hook, landing his fist squarely on That Guy's jaw, who stumbled back in shock. Not wasting a second, Shawn sprinted down Street C, straight towards the horde of zombies that was approaching.

Hurting and rubbing his jaw, That Guy's humour-filled face was replaced with one of hatred and fury. Throwing his shades to the ground, he chased after Shawn with murder gleaming in his dark eyes.

That Guy was faster than Shawn. He pounced straight on top of him and they both collapsed to the ground. Shawn span to face That Guy, but it was too late to dodge out of the way.. Taking several beats, Shawn felt hot blood begin rolling down his face. Unable to see straight, he spat straight up at That Guy, spraying the Asian's face with blood.

They were now surrounded by zombies, but That Guy didn't seem to care. He threw yet another punch, which Shawn managed to avoid, making That Guy land a heavy punch on the pavement as Shawn rolled away.

His enemy spent a moment hurting, gasping in pain at his hand. This allowed Shawn to jump up and kick That Guy straight in the face, shattering his nose. Without slowing down, Shawn pulled two zombies in his direction, hoping they would finish him off.

Sprinting back to the carousel mirrors whilst beating off the many zombies that had arrived on the street, Shawn noticed that That Guy had shrugged off the zombies faster than he'd hoped. After punching the lights out of several partially decomposed zombies, That Guy chased Shawn once again.

"Fucking come here and face me you shit-titan!" he screamed across Street C to Shawn as he ran towards him, still beating off zombies with his bare fists.

Shawn didn't reply, he simply grabbed the red laser pen from his pocket and shone it straight into the carousel mirror. That Guy didn't even notice this as he went straight for Shawn's face once again, landing another hard blow onto his soft, living flesh. Crushed against a house wall and That Guy's fist, Shawn felt a couple of his teeth crack and pop out as though they were abandoning his mouth in fear of being crushed themselves.

Yet again, Shawn spat, making That Guy's already red and angry face even redder and angrier. Unable to see for a moment, a flailed blindly, allowing Shawn time to land a perfect punch in his gut and then another round his blood-soaked chops. That Guy staggered backwards, straight into the hands of a zombie. Hoping once again that the zombie would finish him off, Shawn turned his attention to another approaching zombie, ripping its soft and decomposed legs off and allowing its black blood to trickle into the pools of his own red blood, which was now all over the tarmac.

Despite hurting and his blurred vision, Shawn felt he was winning the fight. And Jeremy and Dustin were on their way. He let out a laugh as he unintentionally spat more blood out of his mouth.

That Guy however, was no pushover. After beating away one of the zombies, he pulled out a machete alarmingly similar to the ones the I Shower Naked Club had acquired off Pesk's goons from a holster on his back and struck down the remaining zombies around him with three clean slices.

"What!?" Shawn couldn't believe what he was witnessing, "Where were you hiding that thing? Up your arse?"

"Uh, yeah, sure, why not?" That Guy replied as though he didn't care what Shawn believed.

"Well in that case, so was I," Shawn smiled, drawing his own machete and chopping down a couple of the nearby zombies, spraying his body with their black blood.

The number of corpses surrounding the two fighters was increasing. The more they took down, the more seemed to stumble upon Street C. While Shawn was distracted, That Guy saw a chance to take him down. Luckily, Shawn heard him approach and turned to block the swipe just in time. Blade ground against blade as the pair both attempted to force the crossed edges into each other's faces. The orange setting sun gleamed ferociously off the blades as they stood in deadlock.

Realising that Shawn was actually stronger than him, That Guy deliberately let his blade slip, causing Shawn to stumble over to one side, allowing That Guy to send two powerful knee-kicks into Shawn's stomach.

Shawn spent a moment coughing up blood as That Guy sent his blade swinging down. Fortunately, Shawn saw this coming and desperately blocked That Guy's killing blow once again. Like pirates, they circled, swinging their machetes around in attack and defence, chopping off the limbs of the zombies as they approached and throwing in as many sly kicks and punches as they could to each other. It was a strange but beautiful dance of teamwork and rivalry as the pair helped each other to take out the oncoming horde of zombies but immediately turning against one another as soon as they could.

"Why are you doing this?!" Shawn spat as he took a swipe at That Guy, who avoided the stinging burn of Shawn's blade by jumping backwards towards a house wall.

That Guy didn't even attempt to reply. He immediately swung his blade out, the tip of his machete clipping Shawn's handle. Shawn watched him horror as his machete spun out of his hand and clattered upon the tarmac a couple of feet behind him.

Showing off his blood red teeth with an evil grin, That Guy approached with the blade spinning in his hand as though he was a drug dealer version of the Prince of Persia. Shawn began backing off, hoping he would be able to get back to his blade. Unfortunately, his attacker lunged in for a swing sooner than he hoped. For a horrible moment Shawn thought he was a goner. Where the fucking hell was Dustin and Jeremy?

Shawn ducked, falling in view of That Guy's shoes. Noticing that That Guy's shoelace was loose, Shawn immediately grabbed the loose lace and pulled. He didn't expect it to have much of an effect, but it was all he could think to do. Surprisingly, Shawn didn't just untie That Guy's shoes, but he also managed to pull the shoe off and send That Guy falling backwards. Shawn saw his chance, it was now or never.

He leaped upon the Renault driver, landing two heavy punches into his face, sending blood splattering in many directions. Attempting to scrabble up the house wall behind him, That Guy fumbled his machete, relinquishing it to Shawn. That Guy stood up to find he was without his blade and stuck against a house wall with an armed Shawn right in front of him.

Shawn pointed the blade right at That Guy's neck, making sure he remained pinned up against the house wall.

This was when Dustin and Jeremy finally showed up, both covered in black blood. Jeremy was holding half of a snooker cue as he pushed Dustin along in the trolley. As well as holding Dustin, the trolley was filled with their makeshift weapons. Dustin pulled out the BB Gun and fired several pellets at a zombie approaching him. The zombie was so soft and decomposed, that the pellet pinged straight through its skull sending it crashing to the floor in a heap of brittle bones and rotten flesh.

"Ha! I won!" Shawn found a laugh to his lips as he stared back at That Guy, "By the way, you're a long fucking guy-"

There was a loud bang, followed by the sound of Shawn's body hitting the floor. Still bleeding, That Guy grinned once again, a smoking gun held in his hands. He had shot Shawn at point blank range, sending his brains scattering out onto the street behind him.

"By the way, I've got a big rectal cavity," That Guy joked, spraying blood from his mouth.

Yet again, there was a nasty silence. Even the zombies seemed shocked at what had just occurred.

"Shit," said Dustin as the pair watched That Guy splutter on his own blood and attempt to walk. They were both surprised to see the dealer was still alive.

"I Shower Naked!" That Guy's grin had gone, as he staggered and shouted across the road towards his car, keeping his gun focused on the pair, "You're coming with me blud!"

"Or what?" Dustin called out to him.

"Or I'll fucking shoot ya, you racist turd clown!" That Guy picked up his blood-soaked shades off the ground as he staggered to his Renault, "Now get in the fucking car blud!"

Jeremy looked around. Zombies had surrounded them and were closing in fast. There was no way of escape. Not without being either being bitten or shot. They had no choice but to get into the car with That Guy.

"Don't make me come over there and get your sorry arses!" That Guy leant on his car door, breathing heavily as he wiped his shades and returned them to his head, the gun shaking in his hand.

Dustin looked at Jeremy and shook his head. Jeremy didn't know what Dustin meant by this, but did the only thing he could. He walked himself and Dustin up to the car. That Guy swung one of the back doors open for them.

"Make sure you leave them weapons in that trolley now," he grinned, humour finding its way back into his voice and facial expression once again, "Famalams be in trouble now."

"Shut the fuck up you dicknose butt mcfaggot!" Dustin's words didn't wipe the bloody grin That Guy was wearing, "Fucking fight me on the street you worthless slut-plug! Let's take it to the curb if you can handle it!"

Sighing, Jeremy picked up Dustin out of the trolley and threw him in the back of the car before tossing his snooker cue into the trolley. Dustin could still be heard firing off racist insults in the back of the car as Jeremy stared at That Guy as he entered the back seats himself.

That Guy chucked once again, keeping his weapon

focused on the pair sat in the back of the car, he checked out their weapon cache. He stared at the museum sword for a while, clearly but found all of the weapons they had unappealing since he simply picked his own machete back up and entered the driver's seat.

"Fucking come at me bro!" Dustin was still roaring away as That Guy locked the car's doors, "I'll take that smug arse smile of yours down yonder motherfucker!"

In a snap flash of fury, That Guy turned around to face Dustin, pulling the gun right to his forehead, "Try it!" he growled, spittle jumping from his mouth and onto Dustin's flesh, "C'mon, man's waiting! In fact I'm begging you so I'll have an excuse to shut that dirty fucking mouth of yours for good!"

Dustin's anger relented. He was still furious and clearly unable to stop shaking or remove the look of hatred in his eyes. That Guy however, chucked once again, turning to relax in his driver's seat.

"What do you want? Where are you taking us?" Jeremy asked as That Guy started his car.

That Guy didn't reply. Instead, he locked the doors and accelerated sharply, sending the car screeching down the road, taking out a few of the oncoming zombies as it did so. Within minutes, Gullum along with their weed supply had disappeared from sight. No spliff for Jeremy and Dustin that night.

DAY 9

That Guy had maintained his silence throughout the entire car journey. The jolt from him accelerating had nearly broke Dustin's neck, or at least it felt that way. His non-existent foot was still hurting too, throbbing as though it was still there, being slowly chewed by zombies. He'd chop it off all over again just to ease the pain, but he knew that was impossible.

Jeremy looked pissed off. Witnessing Shawn's sudden death was probably to blame and the sudden plot twist of having another pre-apocalypse dealer wanting to rain down misery upon them didn't seem to have impressed him.

Dustin stared at their kidnapper through the rear-view mirror. If the shade touting Asian ever once looked back at them he never let on. The sunglasses completely hid his eyes. No clue as to what he was thinking or what he was going to do to them could be gained. That Guy simply sped down Scar Lane, weaving in-between clusters of zombies at breakneck speed. Despite his quite incredible driving skills, skills no doubt perfected in a pre-apocalypse world of being chased by the law, That Guy occasionally collided with the zombies, or other items such as bins, and on one instance the side of a corner shop. This made the ride very rough and the pair in the back bounced around uncontrollably. Dustin wished he had put on his seatbelt as his stump scraped along the side of the car door, causing him unbearable agony.

By the time they had reached Lower Gullum, Jeremy had started attempting to kick the door open, but That Guy took a sharp left towards Puddock, sending Jeremy tumbling across the backseats into Dustin, who howled with pain once again.

By the time Jeremy had pushed himself from Dustin, he was facing That Guy's gun barrel once again.

"TRY IT BLUD!" That Guy roared, not even looking at where he was driving and yet somehow knowing exactly when to steer. Something told Dustin that their local drug dealer had done something like this before.

Jeremy didn't 'try it,' whatever 'it' was. He ceased his assault on the door and That Guy returned his focus back to road. Not that it made much of a difference; Dustin could have sworn he was a better driver with his eyes off the road.

As their mystery journey continued, Dustin found his thoughts returning to his wound. It hurt, a horrible stinging sensation combined with a pulsating ache, it felt like his foot was on fire. He needed another spliff to help with the pain. Or maybe some heroin. Or even a merciful bullet to the head.

That Guy sent the car screaming into Puddock, sending the Renault Clio around the deserted roundabout in a harmonic and orchestral wail of screeching rubber. Half of the tyre rubber was probably left on the tarmac. The car rocked and wobbled like a seesaw, threatening to topple over as he straightened from the roundabout and steamed down a speed-humped road like he was in an illegal street race.

"Aw fuck!" Jeremy moaned as they bounced about the back of the car, as That Guy didn't even acknowledge the existence of speed-humps and dead bodies. Dustin felt his teeth sink into his tongue, feeling pain and tasting the metallic taste of blood.

As Dustin spat blood onto the soft seat material, grinning in pain at the floor of the car whilst they bounced along, Jeremy had taken interest in That Guy's gun. It was nestled conveniently in the mug holder next to the handbrake. A well-timed grab had potential to turn some tables.

That Guy span the wheel as though he was driving a video game and the car rocked to the right as the wheels painfully took it to the left, the decomposing body of a fat dead man splatting against the side of the car and being thrown yards away as though he was being pulled back on bungee cord. Now was his chance. Jeremy grabbed the gun, but instantly regretted the move. He had no idea whether it was loaded or if the safety was on or even how to turn the safety off if it was indeed on.

"Fuckin' wot?" That Guy realised instantly and was not impressed by the move. As Jeremy made a split-second attempt to aim the weapon, That Guy lashed a hand out like an angry snake, instantly grabbing the barrel of the gun and trying to rip it from Jeremy's hands.

Still looking down, it took a knock from Jeremy's flailing arm for Dustin to realise there was a struggle occurring. Ignoring his ailments, Dustin jumped in on the attack, causing That Guy to swerve down the street at great speed, taking out many zombies on the way.

Three people were now prying for a grip on the weapon. Still driving recklessly fast, That Guy pulled viciously, slowly dragging Dustin to the front seat as Jeremy's attempted grip broke.

With Dustin slumped in the front seat, That Guy pulled the gun from his limp grip and laid a heavy pistol whip upon his forehead. The sensation of agony took over Dustin's senses, he even forgot about his missing foot for a moment as his face screwed up with pain like a bulldog sucking on a wasp. A moment later, his nose began bleeding.

Jeremy was desperate not to waste his chances. He instantly wrapped his arms around That Guy's neck, pinning him to the back of his seat and beginning to choke him. A zombie stood gormlessly in the centre of the road was run over, its hideous face pressing up against the windscreen as the lower end of its torso was ripped off and dragged under the car. The car bounced once again and That Guy accidentally shot at the roof.

The noise of the gun startled them all. It ripped through everybody's eardrums. The sound of the world was now nothing but a heavy ringing and the odd feeling that everything was being heard from the bottom of a swimming pool.

"Fuck!" Dustin yelled in the front seat, grasping his ears as Jeremy attempting to continue restraining That Guy.

With his hands now completely off the wheel, That Guy was unable to steer. After ploughing through several reanimated corpses, the car went straight into the side of another corner shop. Sharp shards of glass and wood were thrown in every direction as the car crashed into the already looted shop, tumbling into bare and empty shelves as the car was knocked to its side.

Sideways, and through the pain and cracked windscreen, Dustin saw the end of the shop slide closer as the car knocked through the last of the shelves, finally scraping to a halt just before the final shop window. Above him, That Guy was still struggling from Jeremy's chokehold.

It took a moment for Dustin to realise the car had stopped. Looking through the damaged windscreen, he noticed several zombies were already staggering over to have a gander. With Jeremy and That Guy still fighting it out, Dustin kicked at the windscreen with the only foot he had left in hopes of an escape.

The cracked glass finally gave and the windscreen

shattered, showering himself and That Guy in tiny shards. Not wasting a moment, Dustin pushed himself out of the car, feeling a few sharp shards press into his back. He considered helping Jeremy attack That Guy, but noticed that their kidnapper was actually beginning to win the fight between the two. Maybe he could quietly slide off.

The corner shop they had crashed into was totally trashed. The place was made of broken shelves and shattered glass. Noticing the masses of zombies approaching, Dustin began to crawl his way out of the shop, his stump stinging every move of the way.

Zombies appeared to be ignoring him as he pulled himself over the window frame. They were heading straight for the crashed car, entering the ruined shop through the non-existent door. The sound of Jeremy and That Guy smacking each other from the car was getting louder. He had to move and it had to be fast.

Perhaps Dustin's mistake was that he attempted to stand up. Or perhaps abandoning Jeremy altogether had been the mistake. But he knew he'd blown it when the sound of That Guy climbing from the wreckage was heard. He had only just crawled out of the shop and propped himself up. Not much of an escape.

"Out!" That Guy hissed to Jeremy who was still in the car. He shot two approaching zombies, sending their brain juice splattering against the broken shop. Dustin made an effort to stagger off but the pain in his stump was just too much.

Turning round from the wreckage and That Guy, he was immediately confronted by the mouldy face of a zombie, screaming nonsense at him like some crazed preacher. For a horrible split second, Dustin assumed he was a goner. But That Guy fired once more, taking out the zombie as he dragged a heavily bleeding Jeremy from the back of the car. His shot had been amazingly accurate, dead centre of the forehead, making the zombie crumple to the ground like a sack of bones.

That Guy spat on the ground and instructed the blood soaked Jeremy to move. Neither of them looked happy as the zombies continued to approach. Dustin thought about making a dash for it, but was once again reminded he had a stump for a foot.

Jumping out of his skin, Dustin panicked and ducked when That Guy fired off two more shots. Two more of the approaching zombies slapped on the floor like leaky bags of flour. Dustin glanced back. That Guy was now pointing the gun right at him.

How many shots had he fired? Did he still have bullets? Dustin's mind raced. Once to kill Shawn, once accidentally in the car and five on zombies since that. Seven bullets. Now if he only knew how many was in a clip. Or magazine. Or round. Or whatever.

An angry That Guy marched over to Dustin, dragging Jeremy and a stormy frown with him. Without a word, That Guy slapped Dustin, pistol still in hand. Once again, Dustin found himself blinded by pain.

"Move!"

Dustin found himself being dragged along the street, whimpering as he tried to keep up without applying pressure on his stump. That Guy dragged the pair halfway down the street, making sure they were ahead of the collection of zombies that was in danger of quickly becoming a very large horde.

Within a few minutes they had arrived at an abandoned junior school. The springy concrete that covered the playground was soaked in blood. Pile after pile of rotting corpses rested on top, providing thrilling entertainment for the numerous flies buzzing around like crack addled maniacs. The smell was beyond fowl and as That Guy pulled them through the playground, Dustin noticed that most of the corpses they were passing were children. Grim times.

"In!"

Once again, the pair did as they were told and entered

the school as That Guy held the door open for them. Dustin was getting a little sick of hopping around on one leg. They were taken down a small corridor and into a large hall where class assemblies no doubt occurred once upon a time. Dried blood was smeared all across the wooden floor. It was clear that some poor person had taken it upon themselves to deal with every zombie child in the school. Dustin wondered if it had been That Guy.

The hall had three doors at each side, each one leading to a different classroom. But a classroom wasn't That Guy's destination and he escorted them through the hall to a door that lead to some stairs. It seemed this school had an upstairs.

Dustin found himself saddened as he hobbled through the school. The halls and corridors were jam packed full of displays, boasting the talents of the kids in the form of classroom artwork. Now they were no doubt thrown in the schoolyard with a complimentary bullet in their heads. Or roaming the surrounding areas of Morrhead in the pursuit of fresh meat.

That Guy had turned the upstairs classroom into has base of operations. Unlike the rest of the school, this place had a newer and fresher vibe, nothing but plain white plasterboard walls and a large table full of ammo and weapons. No pictures, no artwork, no sign that this part of the school was even used by the children and its staff. In a back corner was a pile of books that looked inappropriate for children. Dustin noticed one of them was called Blazing Bad.

Without a word, That Guy pushed them both to a corner away from the table. Dustin lost his balance and fell over onto his arse. That Guy put down his blood-soaked shades and picked up some handcuffs and ropes, staring intensely at Jeremy as he did so.

"Well sit down then," he sneered, still staring at Jeremy as though he'd just spilled his pint.

Jeremy sat down slowly and That Guy began tying

them up. The rope was rough and he didn't seem bothered about cutting off blood circulation to vital limbs.

"Look, there is no need for this-" Dustin breathed, attempting to blab his way out of situation as he ignored the stabbing pain from his stump.

That Guy snapped, grabbing a clump of Dustin's hair and pulling his face close for a moment before pushing him back and continuing the tying up. Dustin decided to keep his mouth closed. That Guy was clearly a man of few words and seemed to like it that way.

He forced their backs against each other's and tied the pair up before snapping them on a pair of handcuffs each. Finally, he pulled down the blinds, shutting the room from the last light of the day.

The silence was long as boring as That Guy made little sound at his table of ammunition and weapons, quietly clicking magazines into guns as both Dustin and Jeremy just sat there in silence. Dustin wondered how on zombie-Earth he had acquired so many firearms. About an hour had maybe passed when Dustin made a second effort to communicate with their kidnapper.

"Why are you doing this?"

That Guy didn't even look up or acknowledge Dustin had spoke. He continued his tinkering at the table in darkness.

Dustin glanced at Jeremy behind him, or at least tried to.

"Oi!" Jeremy tried to get his attention. This time it worked.

"Wot?"

"We want some answers," replied Dustin.

"Yeah!" Jeremy agreed.

"Yeah!" Dustin agreed once more.

That Guy appeared to be smiling, or at least that's what it looked like in the darkness. He pulled a gun from the table and a chair from somewhere and sat down, facing them with an amused grin on his face.

"What?" Jeremy asked. That Guy's staring was creeping him out.

"What?" That Guy repeated, a frown forming on his face.

"What are we doing here?" Dustin asked, "I'm guessing you're like the final boss battle or something, is this because we stopped picking up from you?"

That Guy chuckled but shed no information in return.

"He's gone mad or something," muttered Jeremy, "He could be infected too. But I'm deffo seeing crazy in him here."

"What do you want me to say blud!?" That Guy stood up, roaring his face off in the darkness, "'Chaos is the real order' or something clichéd? Ha. Chaos is chaos. Order is the real order. Order of the living that is."

"Well you have your work cut out for you," Dustin replied, "Living is now a very long time unless you have some fatal head trauma."

The rage instantly left That Guy. He began chuckling once again.

"I Shower Naked," he mumbled as he laughed.

The silence crept up once more as That Guy continued his laser-beam stare. Jeremy was about to say something when That Guy began speaking once more.

"You don't get it do you?"

"No."

"You're a joke! You think nobody has been watching you fools try and become badmen just because they're a few dead peeps taking a walk nowadays? You not seen the Twatter group?"

"Twatter group?"

"Yeman," to the pair's surprise, That Guy pulled out a working smartphone, showing off an 'I Shower Naked' page, "Gullum been in stitches over you goon's actions. I mean, you take over idiot Tommy's custom, crashed two cars and a bus into pretty much the same building and somehow kill Pesk's gang and you think no-one would notice?"

Neither of them had anything to say for a moment. Cogs were ticking.

"Twatter group?" Dustin repeated Jeremy's words, "That means, the Internet is still a thing? There is power somewhere? Why didn't we realise?"

"Was a ting," That Guy chuckled, "My 4G died a couple of days ago. Shame, I was enjoying the comments. Can't refresh the page anymore."

"We left our phones at Shawn's yard," Jeremy recalled, "We just sorta assumed zombies would mean the end of the world. Damn, Casper had his craptop too, how did we not know?"

"So... why are you mad at us? We've been taking your customers or something?" Dustin asked.

"Mad at you?" That Guy smiled again, "We ain't mad at you. We love you guys. You've managed to do what we've spent the last six years trying to do in like a few days! You got rid of that yewt Tommy. You got rid of that smackhead Pesk. I'm assuming it was you guys who got rid of Duke as well. Three for the price of one. Can't argue with that, even if you did take my boys Kristoff and Reece as well."

"So..."

"You boys have been getting rid of our competition," That Guy summarised, his dark eyes burning holes in their souls, "And now that you're our only competition, this side of Morrhead will be ours. So thanks boys, you've done us an excellent job."

So much for a climatic ending, Dustin felt a little ripped off by the explanation. He wanted his money back. In fact, he didn't pay any money for this. He wanted his free back. And his foot.

"So what are you gonna do with us? Kill us?" Jeremy asked.

"Yes, no, maybe," he replied, returning his shades to

his head, smiling as though God himself had blessed him.

Dustin shook is head in disbelief. Even Crapital FM had made several mentions of Twatter and yet none of them had put two and two together. Everything they had previously done to survive was beginning to look daft.

"Ah, now ya thinking!" That Guy showed off his bloody teeth once more, "Here's more food for ya thoughts. Ever noticed how we've had nothing but a heat wave since the zombies rose?"

Jeremy shrugged, "So what?"

"So what!?" Dustin frowned, "We live in the bleakest, wettest part of the planet. It rains three hundred days a year usually."

"Exactly," replied That Guy as though the sunshine meant something.

"Well since we're wearing tinfoil hats, I haven't seen any food that hasn't been in a tin," Jeremy retorted sarcastically.

"Exactly," That Guy repeated, "And where did all the ladies go, huh? All the zombies look like guys, innit."

"This is a joke, right?" Jeremy asked as Dustin's mind ticked, "You think there is some sort of huge conspiracy or something?"

"Just sayin' some things don't add up," That Guy rubbed his hands together, "First day, the zombies were running and screaming. Since then, they've stumbled about like drunks."

"That's because they're decomposing!"

"Is it Jeremy? How about that annoying pill bottle somebody always stumbles upon when you're tryin' to keep it low?"

"Yeah, and the clock tower that always chimes at inconvenient times!" Dmitri added.

"Exactly," That Guy said once again, "Things ain't what they seem blud."

Jeremy didn't say anything. The conversation was over. That Guy returned to the indexing of his weapons and ammo or whatever he was doing at the table. The awkward silence returned.

Time slipped away as did what little light was entering the room. With no clock tower in Puddock, there were no regular intervals filled with bells informing them of what time it was. Dustin found himself wondering about their plan. Had it really been so laughable? Had they really been part of the world's first post-apocalyptic joke? He didn't even get the punch line. What was really going on?

Two hours might have passed. Both Dustin and Jeremy had attempted to ask their nameless kidnapper when they were scheduled to die and why it hadn't happened yet. Maybe he was waiting for someone. Or something. Or maybe he just preferred his prey to sweat it out a bit before he did the deed. Either way, the pair were getting bored and impatient. Then there was a clanging noise from outside.

That Guy silently slipped to the window and peeked through the blinds. Dustin and Jeremy saw the bright light of the moon illuminate his eyes and a strip of his face, and he looked as though he'd put on a half-face mask. Whatever it was out there must have got That Guy's attention. In a blink of an eye he had slipped a magazine of bullets into some sort of gun and left the room, as quiet and as nimble as a snake.

This was their chance and both of them knew it. Whatever had happened outside probably wasn't good news for any of them, and being tied up whilst it was occurring wasn't going to improve their chances. It was time to escape.

The first thing they realised was that they couldn't stand up. Dustin had no foot anyway, but That Guy had tied them up so tight that it wasn't possible. Jeremy had made an effort to tense his muscles when That Guy had tied them up, and now with his limbs relaxed, a small amount of room for manoeuvring was made. It was this that was the key to their escape.

A couple of minutes of frantic shuffling occurred, Jeremy attempting to loosen the ropes whilst Dustin made an effort to reach the table of weapons. Being tied together made the situation much more difficult. Being handcuffed didn't help either.

Within a few messy minutes, Dustin had managed to drag them both to the table. Not that it had much use, there was nothing sharp on there from what Dustin could see, which was very little as he was still stuck on the floor.

Jeremy had stumbled upon some luck however. He'd managed to work the loose ropes enough for his leg to slip out. A few seconds later, he jumped out of the loop of ropes, freeing Dustin as he did so. They were still handcuffed, but at least they weren't handcuffed together.

As Dustin hobbled over to the window to take a look at what was occurring. Outside in the monochrome light was That Guy, tackling several zombies with his fists. The zombie count had increased exponentially, the street was literally jam packed full of them and many were tumbling over the wall and into the playground. Beyond that, every street and garden looked packed to the brim with them, going as far as the eye could see. It was a mega-horde. That Guy had no chance of defeating or controlling them and he knew it. After beating several of the zombies off him, he fired out several shots, taking out a few around him, before he slammed the gate shut and sprinted back inside. Literally moments after he had closed the door, the gate swung open once more.

"Shit, he's coming back up," said Dustin, jumping over to the table to find himself a weapon. His hands found contact with a bulky pistol-like weapon, hopefully something like a Desert Eagle as Jeremy hid behind the doorframe for cover.

That Guy entered, obviously not expecting them both to have escaped his ropes. Dustin lifted the gun with his handcuffed arms and squeezed the trigger several times. Several plastic ball-bearings bounced off That Guy's impassive forehead as Dustin realised with horror that he'd grabbed his orange BB Gun.

Blinking heavily and stumbling backwards with surprise slightly, That Guy fired a shot without particularly aiming. The bullet smashed through a table leg and then through Dustin's only healthy leg.

"FUCK!" Dustin screamed as he fell to the floor in another burst of agony. He really wasn't having a good day. The table fell with him, showering him with splinters and loose ammo.

Jeremy jumped from his cover and turned to run as Dustin pocketed his useless BB Gun for some reason. Jeremy's escape looked a success. He sprinted to the stairs, but in his panic, ended up tripping on his own feet and falling down them. With no banister to grab this time, Jeremy tumbled down the stairs and out of sight.

Dustin cursed once more, this time under his breath. The room was dark but not dark enough not to be noticed. Ignoring the pain from both of his legs, he began dragging himself across the floor, slowly and painfully away from his assailant.

There was an ear-splitting bang from behind him, followed by the unmistakable sound of splintering wood. That Guy had missed. There was still chance Dustin could find a working firearm.

"Oh this isn't happening," snarled That Guy, pushing another round into the chamber and taking aim again, "Not on my watch."

His second shot missed again, narrowly avoiding Dustin as he felt the bullet skim his earlobe. His heart was now beating it's way out of his chest. He felt dizzy and sick at the same time, the pain from his legs never once dying, a constant painful reminder that even if he escaped this mess, he's still be in a mess. Where the hell was Jeremy? The staircase wasn't that long.

That Guy marched into the room and fired from a closer range. Wood splintered once more as his ear rang with noise of the gun. A noise of a body slumping down came from behind the upturned table.

Silence took over the piercing bullet shots as That Guy stood in the darkness, only the light ringing of a hollow bullet case to be heard. He had him now. Without making a sound, That Guy righted the upturned table, to be greeted by Dustin's immobile body, leaking blood from several places.

"Ha, I win, just as always," That Guy smiled, turning around.

Before That Guy could even take a step, Dustin span round and leaped up, ignoring his agonizing legs as he stretched his cuffed arms out and around That Guy's neck.

"Guess again fucker!" Dustin spat, pulling on his handcuff chains around That Guy's neck, pulling him over backwards. They both crashed to the floor, Dustin keeping the small length of chain tight around That Guy's neck.

Absorbing his pain, Dustin closed his eyes and focused all of his attention on keeping his hands pulling down on That Guy's neck as hard as he could. That Guy immediately began moving with panic, flailing his arms and legs in every direction to try and free himself from Dustin's chokehold. The dead man's click of an empty gun chamber rang several times as That Guy slammed his fists in every direction, spittle flying out of his increasingly blue lips.

A minute later and That Guy was still struggling for his life as Dustin's arms tried and began to shake. Choking someone to death took longer than he realised, but Dustin's desperation and pain gave him energy. That Guy spat out his final vowels as his life slowly left his body. In one last-ditch attempt to save himself, he flung himself over to try and take the chain pressure off his neck. Unfortunately for him. Dustin was flung over as well, and this time he was able to pull upwards on his chains with even more pressure.

Veins pulsated as fingers writhed and eyeballs swelled.

The last of That Guy's struggle left him, shortly followed by his life. His arms and legs ceased flailing, his fingers and toes an unhealthy shade of blue. His bruised neck dropped his head down, where it hung from the handcuff chain limply.

For the first time in a long time, Dustin breathed. Breathed wasn't the right word. He gasped and gulped the classroom oxygen. He had barely breathed throughout the chokehold and now his lungs had to make up for lost time.

"Oh God..." he mumbled as he collapsed, shaking on top of That Guy's dead body, tears streaming down his face, "OhGodOhGodOhGodOhGod."

It took maybe about minute of anxiety and tears for him to remember Jeremy. He called for him in hope for some help, but no reply came. The sensation of pain was beginning to spread up his legs again. He was still losing blood. It was time to move.

Unhooking That Guy's head from his chains was the first challenge. Dead heads were heavier than he expected, which was surprising since he'd spent just over a week chopping them off bodies. Using his knees as makeshift feet, he shuffled to the staircase.

He carefully slid down the steps on his bottom, one step at a time. The staircase had a curve and once he had turned that, he saw Jeremy's fate.

Jeremy was at the bottom of the stairs, laid on his back, immobile. Dustin assumed he was unconscious at first, but as he got closer the truth became clear. Jeremy had snapped his neck on his tumble down the stairs. He'd been most likely dead before he hit the bottom.

Dustin sat by Jeremy's body for a moment, unable to feel anything but the pain from his legs. No emotion from within, he felt somewhat hollow. He had no idea what to do. Everybody was dead and he had no hope of surviving the outdoor world with two healthy legs, never mind two crippled ones. Despite this particular victory, Dustin didn't feel good at all. He felt tired. He had had enough of the commotion, drama and zombies.

Staring at Jeremy with almost envy, Dustin chuckled. It was only a matter of time before the zombies managed to break into the school, he could hear the distant sound of straining and cracking wood. He could have saved himself a painful death being slowly eaten alive if he hadn't have left the upstairs classroom. It was filled with guns. He was sure he could have found a loaded one to grant himself a peaceful death.

Sure enough, eventually, the sound of the doors collapsing echoed through the assembly hall. A similar sound could be heard from the opposite end of the school. No matter which way he looked at it, Dustin was trapped. Still, there was no need to die like a pussyhole now.

Pulling the orange BB Gun from his pockets, Dustin made sure he had a round loaded. He knew he may as well have been firing flower petals at the zombies, but at least feeling like he was doing something helped.

"Okay then fuckers," he muttered without really moving his mouth, "Bring your best. Or worst. Or whatever. For all the weed and zombies, Zed Wednesday was a good day. Actually no it wasn't, it was horrible."

The first zombie of many turned the corner to face Dustin, its half decomposed face looking like melting wax as it grimaced disgustingly at him. Holding his breath once more, Dustin opened fire.

The End.

ROADBLOC

Previous Books
Vending Machine Lunch.
A Momentary Lapse of Reality.

Social
@roadblochd
www.roadbloc.co.uk